Not the Puck Bunny

Lowball Bay Sea Dragons
Book 1

Freya M. Love

A chance meeting in a quiet corner of a bar leaves me furious, doubting my life choices. Who does he think he is anyway? Just because Cam North is a tall, smoking hot hockey god doesn't mean he can talk to me like that.

I'm done being a doormat for anyone. He was burned before? That's not my problem.

What he doesn't know is who I actually am and why I'm about to make his life a whole lot more complicated.

I have one goal—make the Lowball Bay Sea Dragons ice hockey team as good as I know they can be. To do that, I need to keep a safe distance between me and the players. I can't lose my perspective.

I sure as hell can't lose my heart.

Tropes: Enemies to lovers, hockey romance, boss and employee, workplace romance, mistaken identity, brought together by scandal, secret romance.

Chapter One

Andi

CONTRARY TO POPULAR BELIEF, VODKA DOES NOT, in fact, cure everything.

By 'popular,' I mean my sister, Pia. She means well, but I had to hold the phone away from me to keep her shrieking from having an adverse effect on my eardrums.

I wondered if calling her was such a great idea after all.

"Are you crazy, Andi?" she asked, her voice still in the same high pitch. She tended to question my sanity on a relatively regular basis, so this was nothing new. "The best way to get over a broken heart is to go out and have *fun*."

If anyone knew about broken hearts, it was Pia Welling. She was basically an expert, having left a string of them behind her. I adored her, but she couldn't stick to anything or anyone for longer than a handful of weeks at a time. She changed boyfriends as often as she changed her underwear.

"I wouldn't exactly say it's a broken heart," I said with a sigh. "Xander and I have been growing apart for a long time."

We'd gotten comfortable, like an old pair of scuffed shoes. I thought we'd get married, settle down and live in the suburbs. Have two point five children, a dog and a cat.

All the stuff expected of the elder of the Welling sisters.

That was what I always did. What was expected. If I didn't, I could look forward to that expression of disapproval on Mom's face. She didn't need to give a lecture on responsibility, a glance alone would make most people quiver in their socks.

Dealing with my mother was another on a long list of things vodka couldn't cure.

"He moved out," Pia pointed out. No one would accuse her of sugarcoating anything.

"Two weeks ago," I said.

It wasn't that I hadn't *noticed* he'd moved out, not exactly. It's just... We were so busy, we barely saw each other. I figured, sooner or later we'd bump into each other in the kitchen, or in bed.

Okay, in the back of my mind, I knew he'd gone, but hadn't wanted to accept it.

"Only my sister would fail to notice her boyfriend moved out two whole weeks ago." Pia's tone was drier than the sandtrap in Dad's beloved golf course. "You know what the problem is? You work too much. If you didn't work so many hours—"

"Don't tell me I was too busy to have a proper relationship with him," I interrupted. "He was as absent as I was."

"I was going to say, you would have noticed sooner that he was gone," she said. "What made you realize? The lack of his toiletries in the bathroom? The toilet seat was always down? No one stole the blankets in the middle of the night?"

I cleared my throat softly. "It was Laverne."

Silence.

Then, "Another woman told you?"

I pictured her frowning into her phone, while she walked through the small town of Highball Creek, an hour inland from Lowball Bay, trying to find things to photograph, to add to her portfolio.

I sighed. "No, Laverne is our orchid. Xander was the one who watered her regularly. She started to look dry. I wondered why. Then I realized he wasn't there anymore."

Pia snorted. "I'm sorry, but that is tragic." She sounded like she was holding back a laugh.

"I know, I know, but the word you're looking for is *pathetic*. He and I should have been able to talk about this before he just packed up and left. Am I that unapproachable?"

"Um..."

I rubbed my temples with my fingertips. "That would be a yes." Ouch. "I'm busy, okay? Welling is expanding so quickly, I can't take off and have a break whenever I feel like it."

Our father was CEO of Welling Developments, one of the biggest real estate developers in the state. He built it from the proverbial ground up. It was his passion and his legacy. He passed that same drive on to me.

I was proud to work with him, in my own, tiny office, with my personal assistant. Someday, I'd take over from him. My father, not my assistant.

Rafe would have found this whole situation hilarious. Too many times he'd told me I worked too much and should spend more time practicing my blow job skills.

"Of *course* you can," Pia said. I could almost feel

her eye-roll through the phone. "Tomorrow is Friday. I'm coming down to the Bay and we're going out. You need to have fun, and drink too much of that vodka we were talking about."

"*You* were talking about vodka," I reminded her. "I was saying I don't need to go out. I have a million things to do—"

"Andrea Clarissa Welling, you're coming out with me whether you like it or not." She sounded like our mother. "You need this and I want to spend time with my sister. If you won't do it for yourself, then do it for me."

"Why do you need a night out?" I turned away from my ten foot long kitchen island, towards the view over Lowball Bay.

Recently named one of the fastest-growing, most livable cities on the east coast of the continental United States, my father's company developed at least half of it. It went from a seaport to a cosmopolitan city in a couple of decades. You couldn't walk around downtown without practically falling over an on-trend restaurant, or gallery. The waterfront precinct was one of my favorite places to be. And, let's face it, be seen.

"Because I haven't seen you for weeks," she said. "When was the last time we did anything fun?"

"The last time you were here, we went to the beach," I said. I was reaching here and we both knew it.

"Riiight. Where you got so burnt you looked like a lobster," she said, with unapologetic amusement.

"Thanks for the reminder." My sarcasm was equally unapologetic.

I swear I applied at least fifty layers of sunscreen. Being a pale-skinned redhead, the sun laughed hysterically at my attempts and burnt me to a crisp anyway. Next time, I was wearing clothes from head to toe. Or maybe I'd stay inside.

Pia was the lucky one, with dark hair and skin that tanned more quickly than it burned.

"You're welcome," she said brightly. "Going out is much safer than going to the beach. Less chance of stepping on a jellyfish."

"It wasn't a jellyfish." I unlocked and slid open the door that led to my balcony, shivered at the icy breeze that blew inside and, closed the door again.

"Riiight," she dragged the word out again. "It was a condom."

"Yes. Yes it was." It had squelched under my foot, cold and squishy. I hopped straight off it and let out a squeak of disgust. Without stopping to think, and with Pia howling with laughter behind me, I'd run straight for the water to wash my foot. It didn't feel clean again for days afterward. Even after several showers and a bath, I could feel it there, under my heel.

I shuddered at the memory.

I'd gone to my doctor and got tested for every fuck-knows-what that might have come out of that abandoned piece of latex. Nothing, fortunately.

Like everything else in life, in *my* life anyway, Pia found it hilarious.

"At least your foot didn't get pregnant," she said with a laugh.

"I told you that you should have studied more science at school," I said. "If you had, you'd know feet can't get pregnant."

"Not human feet anyway," she agreed.

"What animal can... You know what, never mind." I shook my head. "Even if that is a thing, I don't want to know about it." How in the world had we gotten to the topic of pregnant feet?

"Don't be such a prude," she scolded playfully. "You never know what you might learn. For example—"

"I'll hang up on you," I warned.

She laughed. "You wouldn't do that to me. You love me too much. That's why I'm coming down there tomorrow and we're going out. We're going to find a hot guy for you to hook up with, to help you forget Xander. That could be your used condom on the beach on Saturday morning."

"I can't even begin to tell you what's wrong with that," I said. "Let's start with the fact that littering is illegal, bad and icky, and it's too cold to have sex on the beach."

"Depends how cold your partner is," she said. "We'll find one hot enough that—"

"I have an idea, how about you concentrate on your own love life?" I said. "Mom is starting to worry you're never going to give her a grandchild."

"What about you?" Pia asked.

"I have Laverne," I said. "Best damn grandplant this side of Highball Creek."

Pia snorted so loud I had to pull my phone away from my ear again. "Grandplant my ass. If that was all it took, I'd be rolling in grandbabies for her. Out here, she could take her pick."

I pictured the wide open countryside, mountains to the west. Clear air and a relaxed pace of life. Sometimes I envied her. Then I remembered I could have a cheeseburger ordered and delivered to my door within an hour. The city came with certain luxuries. That perk was one of my favorites.

"That will never be good enough for her," I said. "You know what she's like. She's about as subtle as a..."

"Wart right in the middle of your ass cheek?" Pia suggested.

"Sure, let's go with that," I said. "I'm assuming you have a lot of experience with this particular medical condition?"

"No, but in high school I went out with a guy that did," she said. "Remember Kyle Coleman?"

"Yes I do, and I don't want to think about his ass cheeks." I grimaced. "And I really don't want to know how you know what his ass cheeks looked like."

The last time I saw him, he was a typical, gangly teenage boy with acne and a high-pitched laugh that sounded more hyena than human. If I remembered right, he didn't have much of an ass to speak of. Not compared to me. I'd always been curvy. Not to mention self-conscious as hell.

"Skinny-dipping," she said anyway. "Right after prom. A whole bunch of us went down to the lake. After a few shots of cheap tequila, it seemed like a really good idea."

I remembered that. Or specifically, I remembered hearing about it. I was away at college at the time, still getting over missing my own prom. My date broke up with me the day before, so he could take one of the cheerleaders instead. I decided not to go, and stayed home binge eating chocolate ice cream, while watching reruns of *Buffy the Vampire Slayer,* and hugging my plush vampire.

Don't judge me, that vampire got me through all those years of high school. Lucky for everyone, he couldn't talk, because I'd told him all the secrets I'd never tell anyone else. Not even Pia. Right now, he was tucked away in the back of my closet. If my mother knew he was there, she'd be horrified. Several times, she'd tried to throw him in the trash, only to have me pull him back out again. Count Bob—I was eight when I named him, okay—deserved better.

Pia left a string of broken hearts behind her, but all I seemed to have was a string of disappointments that always equated to the same thing. I was never good enough, no matter what I did. At work, yes, but not in love.

I'd settled for Xander, when I knew we weren't compatible in the short term, much less for the rest of our lives. Maybe I'd meet some hot guy and hook up for wild sex, but I wasn't going to get involved with anyone. Not again.

From now on, I'd focus on my job and trying to

keep Laverne alive. If I couldn't look after a plant, then I had no business trying to look after anyone else.

"Fine," I said finally. "Let's go out tomorrow night. I can tell you all about the new project Dad put on my desk. You won't believe it."

Chapter Two

Cam

Contrary to popular belief, beer doesn't solve everything.

Try telling that to my best friends and teammates.

I trailed behind them through the wide doorway and into Shells. The bar was packed full of players from the Lowball Bay Sea Dragons, their wives, girlfriends and more puck bunnies than I could swing a stick at. A band was setting up in the corner. Any moment now, we'd be elbow to elbow, shouting to be heard over them.

Just what I needed tonight.

Not.

"Good game tonight," Brody Clutterbuck, the owner of Shells, greeted us. "Nice assist, Cam."

I nodded my thanks and stepped over to the bar to order a light beer.

"When are you going to get that stick out of your ass?" Nate Southwell leaned on the bar beside me. He grimaced and raised them, the elbows of his shirt dripping from the moisture in the bar mat.

Blake Eastwood, who stood on the other side of him, chuckled.

Nate flipped him off. He shook out his arms and pushed his sleeves up, revealing an expanse of tattooed skin. For some reason, women went crazy for his ink. And him. The defenseman practically fought them off every time we went out. Practically, because he wasn't trying very hard.

If I had to guess, I'd say he'd been with three hundred and sixty-five different puck bunnies in the last year.

Whatever, that was him. Let people flock to kiss his ass. Me, I was the brooding giant in the background. The way I liked it.

"Lay off Cam." Flynn Weston, the team's center, cast a sidelong glance at Nate. He didn't say much, but when he did, he was usually telling Nate to shut up. As far as I could tell, he was the only one who could keep the defenseman in line. The rest of us gave up trying a long time ago.

"What?" Nate shrugged. "I'm just saying he needs to loosen up a little. Don't tell me I'm wrong. You're both thinking it." The pretty blonde behind the bar placed a beer in front of him. He winked at her before turning to toast them, and took a sip.

She blushed before wilting slightly under the look I gave her. She hurried to pour my beer before I pointed out I'd ordered mine first.

"She must be new," Blake remarked. "Most of the women here have become immune to Nate's charms."

I waited until Nate took another sip and said, "You mean he's slept with the rest of them and they've discovered he's only in it for a few minutes."

He choked on his beer, coughing until his face was as pink as the woman's behind the bar.

I smiled behind my glass before taking a much more careful sip.

"I last longer than a few minutes," he protested.

"You have enough witnesses to that," Blake teased.

Nate shrugged, completely shameless. "At least I don't pretend I'm in it for the long term. With me, women know exactly what they're getting. One night of bliss that will ruin them for every other man."

I snorted into my drink.

"If you got your head out of your ass, you could find out what it's like," Nate said to me.

"My head isn't up my ass, and you're not my type," I deadpanned.

He took the bait. "I meant you could find bliss with multiple, beautiful women. At the same time if you wanted to."

I'd had my share of puck bunnies. Like a lot of guys, when I signed with the NHL, I was happy to accept any and every offer that came my way. And they came my way often. So often, they started to blur together, until every encounter became increasingly meaningless. I stopped bothering to ask for names, knowing I wouldn't remember them later.

That lifestyle was fine for Nate, but I was over it. I fucked around less and less these days. Partied less too. Spent more time thinking about life after hockey. That thought was depressing as hell, but we all had to face it sooner or later.

"And deprive them of your company?" I said. "What sort of friend would I be if I did that?"

"The kind who gets laid?" Blake suggested.

I smirked at him. I didn't need him piling on me as well.

"There's nothing wrong with not wanting to fuck anything that lies still for long enough," Flynn said.

"Exactly." I nodded.

Needing some space, I stepped away from them and headed to the lounge area at the back of the bar.

Several long couches lined the walls, tables in front of them. Above the couches, hung photos of past and present members of the Sea Dragons. Alongside those were photos of the Sea Cucumbers, Lowball Bay's baseball team, and the Humpbacks, the NFL team. At the end was a collection of photos of the Starfish, the local NBA team.

In the center of the lounge, leather armchairs surrounded low, round tables with tops scuffed by time and stained with rings from drinks left too long. The decor was classic and well loved, rather than tacky and tired.

As usual, the lounge was occupied by the players who weren't single, and their wives and girlfriends. The single players and bunnies tended to avoid the lounge, at least this early in the night.

I slid into an armchair as the band started up with a cover of *Welcome to the Jungle*. The drumming would give me a headache, but they could have been worse.

Flynn lowered himself into the seat beside me. "Don't let Nate or Blake get to you. They're still out to live their best fuck boy lives. We were both like that a few years ago."

I crossed my knees and leaned back. "I was never like Nate." I was popular enough, but women didn't fall on my cock the way they did his.

Flynn raised an eyebrow at me. "That's not how I remember it." He held up a hand before I could protest. "I'm not judging you, dude. But something got to you. If you ever want to talk about it—"

"I don't," I said bluntly. "It's not important now."

He gave me a skeptical look.

"It really isn't," I insisted. "I just decided that lifestyle wasn't for me. Can a guy not change without being questioned?"

"Yes," he said slowly. "If you weren't a friend and teammate. You're the best winger the Sea Dragons have. If you're having trouble with anything, I wouldn't be much of a captain if I didn't ask."

"I'm not having trouble with anything." My tone was stonier than I intended. "Give it a rest, okay?" I downed the last of my beer and stalked off to the bar for a refill.

I half expected Flynn to follow, but he didn't. He meant well, but I genuinely had nothing to say. Nothing that wouldn't have him judging me. Right now I was doing plenty of that to myself, I didn't need him doing it too.

In the corner of my eye, I caught a curvy redhead, whose curls bounced around her face as she walked. She wore a sage green sweater, made out of mohair or something expensive-looking. Her blue jeans accentuated her curves.

"See, this is perfect." She was with a brunette in a bright pink sweater and black leggings.

The redhead pressed her pink lips together, flattening out her Cupid's bow for a moment before she reluctantly smiled. One of her bottom teeth was slightly crooked, the rest were white and even.

"I never would have figured you for the sports bar type, Pia," the redhead said. Judging by the resemblance, I guessed they were sisters.

"Anywhere there's alcohol and hot guys is perfect for my big sister," Pia replied, confirming my guess. "Come on, have a few drinks and lighten up. And while you're at it, take a look around. We seem to have stumbled into hot guy central."

I curled my lip and looked away.

'Stumbled on,' my ass. I knew a pair of puck bunnies when I saw them. It was only a matter of time before Nate spotted them and took at least one of them home, possibly both. He'd love a threesome with two cute sisters.

If I missed my guess, the redhead might need some persuasion from Pia, but that was one thousand percent *not* my problem.

I sipped my beer, my attention half on the replay of tonight's game that was playing on the screen behind the bar.

I'd never get used to seeing myself skate like that. Ever since I was a kid, the only dream I had was to play for the NHL. I used to play pond hockey with my brother Griffin and sister Alice. To them, it was fun. To me, it was completely serious.

I could barely tie the knot on my skates, but I was training for my future.

My teachers used to tell me to focus on a more realistic goal, but the only goals I saw were biscuits sliding into baskets. Nothing else held my interest.

Seeing that dream come to life a decade ago, still didn't seem real to me. I was living little Cameron Michael North's wildest fantasies. There were still mornings where I rolled out of bed for morning skate and pinched myself. The long hard days, and nights were worth every drop of blood, sweat and tears.

The whole bar seemed to stop and watch as I made the assist that led to Flynn scoring the goal which won us the game. The place erupted in cheers, but I kept my eyes on the screen until the ad break.

I placed my empty glass on the bar and headed to the restroom.

As I stepped back out into the cacophony of sound, and the smell of stale alcohol, I bumped into someone heading the other way.

It took me a second to process that moment of heat and soft impact was the curvy redhead. I shuffled back, out of her space, as far as the narrow corridor would allow. It wasn't far. Even pressed against the wall, there was barely enough room for two people.

"Shit, sorry." She looked flustered, her curls falling over her blue eyes. She pushed them back and blinked at me a couple of times. Her lashes matched her dark red hair. Did they match the hair at the apex of her thighs?

What the hell? I asked myself.

I managed to keep my eyes on her face and not dip down lower.

"Are you okay?" She peered at me, looking concerned.

"Yeah, I'm fine," I said, realizing I was staring.

Very smooth, Cam. My inner voice snorted at me.

I told it to fuck off. "You good?"

"I'm fine," she said. "I should have been looking where I was going."

Her voice was low and husky. My balls decided now was a good time to take notice. I told them to shut up too. They'd get me into trouble if I let them.

"Sure," I said, half under my breath. As if pretending to run into someone wasn't the oldest puck bunny meet-cute in the book.

Yes, I know all about meet cutes; my sister reads a lot of romance novels. I won't admit to having borrowed them from her shelves, and read them before sneaking them back into place. No way.

Okay, yes I had, and I wasn't ashamed of it. I just wouldn't admit it if someone like Nate asked. There were things about me he didn't need to know. Mostly because he'd tease me mercilessly and there was nothing wrong with men reading romance novels. It was a good way to learn what women wanted without having to test that on a different woman every night.

He had his methods, and I had mine. I stood by it.

"I don't even know what I'm doing here," she admitted. "This was all my sister's idea. She thinks I need to get out more."

"Right." I started to step around her. It sounded to me like her sister had a lot in common with Nate. No doubt they'd get along perfectly. That was also not my problem.

She stepped sideways with me. "Can I buy you a drink to apologize for running into you?" She held out her hand for me to shake.

I looked down at it and kept my hands by my sides. Apparently I needed to make my lack of interest clearer. She was gorgeous, but it was better if I walked away right then. Better for me and for her.

"I don't fuck puck bunnies." I might as well be honest with her, before she made any assumptions, or further attempts to get my attention. Some women didn't like to take no for an answer. I'd save us both the hassle and nip this in the bud before it grew into a clingy weed.

She blinked again. She must have been an excellent actor, because she seemed genuinely confused. "Excuse me?"

I looked at her coldly. Before she could say another word, I placed my palm on the wall behind her. Leaned in until my breath brushed her pale, freckled cheek. Her breasts were almost touching my chest. I ignored the way her breathing became faster and shallower.

Her hair smelled like lavender. My grandmother used to dry the stuff and put it in teddy bears to sell at the local market. Somehow the scent made her seem, I don't know, innocent. I wanted to tell her to get the hell out of Shells. Stay away from players before she got played.

Instead, I whispered in her perfectly shaped ear, "I. Don't. Fuck. Puck. Bunnies."

I pushed myself off the wall and stalked away, out of the bar.

Chapter Three

Andi

My practical heels clicked on the white tiled floor.

I glanced down before skirting around the Sea Dragons' logo laid in the center, between panes of glass that bracketed the tall front, sliding doors.

Everyone else, I noticed, walked straight across it, wearing a path on the colored section of flooring. I winced to myself. The adorable Ruby Sea Dragon mascot, Cee-cee, was too cute for me to step on.

Us redheads have to stick together, I told her silently. She looked back at me, smiling and marketable. Cee-cee merchandise was a big revenue stream for the team. T-shirts, hoodies and plushies like the one I saw on the screen at Shells nearly a week ago.

A kid was waving her in the air, celebrating the win. That was right before that dark-haired asshole with ice cold brown eyes got all in my face. Mistaking me for someone who only wanted to sleep with hockey players to boost their public image, or whatever.

I wouldn't judge another woman for her life choices, but it wasn't something I'd do. Besides, everything I knew about ice hockey would fit in the back of a postage stamp.

Were those even things anymore? I thought so, although they'd largely been replaced by electronic communication and barcodes.

That man though. The memory made my pulse involuntarily race with a combination of irritation and arousal. Mostly irritation. Who did he think he was anyway?

Okay, I admit it. For approximately three seconds, I thought he might be exactly what I needed to help me forget about Xander. Right before he got up close and shattered that illusion. If I wanted an arrogant asshole, I'd date one of approximately half the men from Dad's office. Too many of them would happily date the boss's daughter, in the hopes it would boost their career.

Exactly why I had no intention of dating anyone I worked with. That was all way too muddy.

I stopped at the wood-clad reception desk and smiled at the woman who sat behind it, her hair wound in a neat, pink bun.

I showed her my I.D.

Her eyes narrowed, then widened. She shot up, sitting straighter in her seat. The sudden movement made it roll back a couple of feet, almost into the wall behind her. She windmilled her arms before pulling herself forward again with the ball of her feet.

"Ms. Welling! Head Coach Lampton and the rest of the team are waiting for you. I'm Ursula." She stuck out her hand. Manicured, bright pink nails matched her hair.

I leaned forward to shake her hand. "It's nice to meet you, Ursula."

I always made a point of remembering the names of people I worked with, especially those who worked in reception, or as assistants. They seemed to appreciate the effort, and in return, they were more accommodating when I needed anything done. Besides, I didn't want to be one of those faceless CEOs no one could approach without wanting to pee their pants.

"If you don't mind me asking, Ms. Welling..." Her blue eyes were tentative behind long lashes that looked real.

"Please, call me Andi," I said. "I don't foresee any big changes. At least, not right away. Your job is safe. As long as you keep doing it to the best of your abilities." Ugh, now I sounded like my mother. I smiled, hoping it didn't look like I was the one who suddenly needed to pee.

She smiled and visibly relaxed. "I always do, Ms.... Andi. If you need anything, just give me a shout."

"If you could point me to where the team is waiting?" I hadn't stepped foot in the arena before. I hadn't expected to. Not before my father dropped this in my lap five days ago.

I knew what this was. A test in the form of a gift. If I could run an ice hockey team, I could add it to my resume. When it came to choosing his replacement as CEO, it'd set me apart from other prospective candidates.

Why an ice hockey team? I had no idea. Probably because he was well aware I knew absolutely nothing about the sport. He was generous at throwing me in at the deep end.

I was determined not to drown. I also needed to

stop thinking about water, or I'd need a pit stop at the toilet.

"Of course," Ursula said, her tone perky. She stood and led me over to a bank of elevators. "Third floor. When you get out, turn left, then turn right. Go all the way to the end of the corridor and you'll see the meeting room. They'll be in there."

"Not out on the ice?" According to a sign beside one of the elevators, the rink was downstairs from the reception desk, to the rear of the building. Beside the massive public car park.

"Shouldn't they be training or something?" I didn't want to disrupt their routine. Assuming they had one. Was that a thing with sporting teams? I presumed it was, otherwise their days would be in disarray. If there was anything I hated, it was disarray.

"Not for this meeting," Ursula said. "This is a big deal. We've been speculating ever since your father bought the Sea Dragons. After the last owner, the guys were nervous. I mean, who bets against their own team?" She made a face.

Probably someone who saw the Sea Dragons' loss record last season. That was a thought I'd keep to myself. I got it, morale wasn't great around here.

That was one of many items on my list to rectify, if I could.

"Someone who's in the team's past," I said. And good riddance. "As evidenced by the Sea Dragons' win the other night."

Ursula beamed. "They did so well," she enthused. "Especially Cam and Flynn."

"Cameron North and Flynn Weston," I said, picturing the team roster I'd spent yesterday memorizing.

Ursula's smile broadened. "Yes, them. They've both been superstars in the pre-season. Along with Nate Southwell and Blake Eastwood. They're tight off the ice too, the four of them. Like brothers, even if the family is slightly dysfunctional."

I committed all of that to memory. "What family isn't a little dysfunctional?" I said with a slight laugh.

Her smile didn't falter. "Mine certainly is. But I've kept you for long enough. I'm so sorry!"

"Don't be," I said easily. "It's nice to know the inner workings of the team."

"The gossip, you mean," she admitted.

I smiled. "Gossip has its place. I expect you'll keep me up-to-date with all the gossip I need to know."

"If you need gossip, I'm your girl." She nodded

and hurried back to her desk as another person approached.

I pressed the up button and waited for the elevator. The bank contained three of them, apparently all of which were currently at level four.

I tapped my toes on the floor and waited while they remained at level four. I pressed the up button again, for extra oomph, as if that would get me there sooner, and kept waiting.

Finally, the elevator on the right started to move. Up to level five.

"Of course," I said under my breath.

The elevator on the left moved down to level three, before returning to level four.

"Okay, I get the hint." I started to look around for a set of stairs I could take instead.

My mother would remark that I needed the exercise anyway. I told her voice in my head to shut up. If only I could do that in person.

"Have you tried pressing the button?" A young man in a suit stopped beside the elevator. He pressed the up button with the tip of his finger. The center elevator door immediately opened with a happy ping.

He gave me a look like he was doubting my

sanity, before gesturing for me to step into the car first.

To be honest, I was questioning my sanity too, but I stepped past him and pressed the button to take me to the third floor.

With any luck, it would actually stop there. Otherwise, I might discover exactly what the attraction of level four was.

If I recalled correctly, it was just office space up there. Hell, for all I knew, they'd turned it into a videogame arcade. If that was the case, I looked forward to seeing it for myself.

Lucky for me, my elevator companion only needed to go to level two. He kept his distance as far as the car would allow, before giving me another funny look and quickly stepping out and away.

"First order of business," I said when the doors closed behind him. "Getting these elevators looked at. Second order of business, stop talking out loud to myself."

I glanced at my reflection in the shiny walls of the elevator car and patted my hair down as best I could. My curls were as obedient as the elevator system.

I'd tried straightening them, and even wearing my hair short, but it always bounced back into a riot of wild curls. Not even an anti-frizz conditioner helped it to settle.

In the end, I gave up and wore it in a ponytail or a messy bun. If it was going to look messy, I might as well try to convince people it was deliberate.

By some miracle, the elevator stopped at the third floor. The door actually opened. I even clicked out into the corridor without tripping and falling on my face. Things were looking up. For now.

I looked both ways with a frown. Ursula had said to turn left, hadn't she? I nodded to myself, before going that way, then taking a right.

A long corridor, lined with doorways led to ordinary offices. On the western side, they showed sweeping views of the city of Lowball Bay. To the east, the offices had views of the sparkling ocean.

I hurried down the corridor toward the sound of voices. They sounded relaxed, friendly. Chatty banter and the occasional laugh.

"Shut up, Nate," called out a cheerful voice. "You know it's not..."

I couldn't make out the rest of what he said, he'd lowered his voice.

"Whatever," someone else replied. "They won't keep us waiting much longer. They know how important we are."

That was met with a chorus of laughter.

"If you say so, Nate," a rumbly male voice said.

"What did you say their name was, Coach?" I thought that might have been Nate. "Andrew Welling. How bad can he be?"

I winced.

This wasn't the first time people got confused. I preferred to go by Andi, rather than Andrea, for a whole bunch of reasons.

Firstly, imagine an angry mother shouting out, "*Andreaaa*," in a shrill voice. That explains at least half of it. The rest of it— I liked Andi. It was a no-nonsense name that suited me, a no-nonsense person.

Okay, that was the image I tried to portray to the world. My hair, and tendency to step on things I shouldn't, told a different story. Expectations versus reality weren't always kind.

I stopped in the doorway that led to the huge meeting room.

Being right at the back of the building, the view out the windows showed the city and a stretch of glittering waves. The arena was on prime real estate.

I'd wondered if my father wanted to tear it down and build apartments on the land, but I suspected he would have had a fight on his hands if he tried.

Regardless of their performance, the city loved its team and its arena. Besides which, the arena was good for the local economy. Even my father couldn't argue with that, in spite of the impact on his bottom line. He was a businessman before he was anything else, and good will went a long way to getting things done quickly and to his advantage.

The room itself had gray carpet, the logo of the Sea Dragons on the wall, and more chairs than I could count.

If I had to guess, I'd say the entire roster was here in the room, not just the first line, and all of the coaching staff, from the head coach, to the goalie coach and strength and conditioning coach.

There was more testosterone in this room than there was in Shells Bar the other night. More testosterone than in my father's office building. A couple of the coaches were women, but the rest, and all the players present were men.

That was another order of business. A women's hockey team for the Lowball Bay Sea Dragons.

For now, I'd deal with what was in front of me. If I could.

Wait.

Shit.

I stared in disbelief.

The asshole from Shells leaned his hip against the table in the corner. He looked at me with those same cold, brown eyes. This time, they were laced with a measure of confusion.

"Take a wrong turn?" he asked before anyone else realized I was there.

"I don't think so," I said as brightly as I could manage. "I'm the team's new owner, Andi Welling."

Chapter Four

Cam

SHIT.

Shit.

I recognized that pale skin. The wild, red curls. The curves now clad in a pencil skirt that fell halfway down shapely calves. A bright blue sweater covered her perfect breasts. In heels, she didn't come up much past my chin.

Those same brilliant blue eyes, so warm and apologetic before I shot her down the other night, were now colder than the ice on the rink. Her tone was smoother than after the Zamboni did its magic.

Her plump lips set in a line upon seeing me. No chance she didn't remember me.

Zack Reed snorted loudly. "New owner's secretary?"

I bristled at his derisive suggestion. He hadn't evolved far from Neanderthal in his thinking. The team worked on that with all of us. Some of us even pulled it off once in a while. Zack refused to try.

Andi turned that ice cold gaze on him, before smiling in a way that made me glad she wasn't looking at me. "The word you're looking for is personal assistant, and no, I assure you, I'm the team's owner, Mister—?" She cocked her head.

Zack grunted, irritation flashing across his face. He was used to people knowing exactly who he was.

Did Andi really not know, or was she trying to bring him down a peg or two? Had she recognised me at Shells? I assumed she had, and had walked into me on purpose. But now... I wasn't so sure.

She blinked at him a couple of times, her long lashes almost brushing her cheeks.

Zack stood straighter than the blue line. "Zack Reed. Winger."

"Ah, I see." She straightened her head and nodded, like she didn't have a clue about any of the five positions on the ice. The keen intelligence in her eyes said otherwise. She was humoring him, but making him look like an idiot at the same time.

Like he needed help with that.

Beside me, it was Flynn's turn to snort. He wasn't fooled either.

Zack shook his head as if he didn't know what was going on, but didn't like it. He shot her a dark look, then lounged back against the wall, arms crossed over his chest. His gaze followed her every move as she spoke to the head coach.

"Brian Lampton." He offered her a smile and his hand. He actually winced at her grip, but nodded his approval. "The team's been curious to meet you." He raised an eyebrow, adding further meaning to otherwise benign words.

She reclaimed her hand. "I'm sure they have."

I didn't imagine her gaze sliding in my direction, before flicking back to Coach. What did that mean? Did she think *I* knew who she was the other night? I frowned, trying to make some sense of it. I was missing something, that was obvious. Who was this woman?

I glanced at the guys. Blake and Nate shrugged. Flynn's expression gave away nothing.

Andi cleared her throat and addressed the room. She didn't raise her voice any louder than a normal, conversational level. She knew how to make herself heard without shouting.

That further added to the mystery of who she

was. If she owned a hockey team, she must have money, maybe even influence.

Another good reason to stay away from her. Women like her didn't look twice at men like me. She probably ate caviar off gold plates, and had black silk sheets. I was not going to picture her eating caviar off a gold plate while lying naked on those silk sheets. My dick was certainly *not* going to twitch at the idea.

She was trouble with heated, silver toilet seats, or whatever people like her had.

Something about Andi Welling suggested she wasn't like that, but I'd been fooled before. I wasn't letting a pretty face fool me ever again.

My balls reminded me how it felt to be close to her, her lips inches from mine. I ignored them. Thinking with my balls never ended well.

They both stuck up their middle fingers at me. Figuratively.

"I don't intend to make any major changes," Andi was saying. "Not right away. Except for the elevators. They seem a little janky."

"They are janky," Nate offered. "You need to hold down the button *hard* before they play nice." His choice of words were deliberate. "If you like, I can show you around the arena." He wore his best, smooth-as-fuck expression on his face.

For some reason, I wanted to wipe it right off there.

"That would be nice, thank you," she said graciously. "Unless anyone has any questions for me?" Up until now, we'd kept the muttering between ourselves to a minimum, but the speculation was undeniable.

"How come you own a hockey team?" Blake asked, forward as ever.

She smiled at him, like she expected the question. "Why wouldn't I own one?"

"Okay, why *this* one?" Blake pressed. "I mean, we're awesome and all, but..."

"Does it bother you that a woman owns your team?" Her expression was bland, but her words laced with expectation. Of what, I wasn't sure. She seemed to want his honesty.

"Nah," he replied easily. "Anyone who doesn't know Zack is all right in my books."

"Fuck off," Zack growled. "She doesn't know who you are either." He glared at Blake, hands in fists at his sides.

Blake grinned back at him, undeterred. "I'm okay with that. She will soon."

"Blake Eastwood," Andi said, her tone still bland, but something like mischief shining in her eyes. "Goalie."

Blake grinned bigger, while Zack spluttered.

Nate and Flynn both choked back laughs, and even Coach Lampton was smiling.

Me? I wasn't sure what to think. Did she know who we were or didn't she?

"Lucky guess," Zack muttered.

"Blake is one of the most recognized players in the NHL," I stated, my gaze on hers, watching for her reaction.

"Point nine one zero save average," Andi said, her chin raised.

"It could be better." Blake rubbed a hand over the back of his head and tried not to crow at being singled out.

"So, you know who we are," I stated.

"Some of you," she admitted. "I did some research. Others, I might have met under other circumstances." Her voice was sweet, but her gaze was dusted with venom.

"Yeah." My gaze slid away from her.

In the corner of my eye, I caught Zack smirking, certain she'd called me out somehow. Equally certain I deserved it. Maybe I did. Maybe I didn't.

Just because she owned the team didn't mean she wasn't a puck bunny. People with too much money did all sorts of weird things, including buying a hockey team so they could screw around with the players. If that was her angle, I missed a major bullet by refusing her invitation the other night.

I reminded myself she'd only offered me a drink to apologize for colliding with me. That was where it started. And ended. It had to. Even if I was interested in seeing her lying naked on my bed, her legs apart so I could taste her pussy, she was my boss.

If my balls could laugh, they'd be doing that right now. Or maybe crying, because they were very interested in getting closer to her. My cock was taking sides as well. He agreed with my balls.

I'd have to be careful to think with my brain. No matter what the rest of me thought, I could never go there with her. Besides, it was clear she hated my guts. That would make staying away a lot easier.

"So, about that tour..." Nate said.

"I'll do the tour," Coach said. "You guys should be down in the rink, training."

Nate only looked slightly put out. He smiled at Andi and even gave her a wink. "I'm sure we'll catch up soon."

"I'm sure we will," she said, inclining her head

towards him. She didn't seem interested, but she wasn't giving him the brush off either.

Why did I care? I didn't. Unless something happened between them which had a negative impact on the team. Yeah, that was it. It had nothing to do with my cock wanting to stand up like the needle on a compass, pointing due North, right at her.

It's just physical, I told myself. There was no denying she was cute, or that I wanted to touch her curves, or look up at her while she bounced on my cock, breasts bouncing with her...

If I continued this line of thought, I was going to leave this room with a boner.

My balls had been complaining about the lack of action for a while. That was the only reason they were causing me problems now. It had nothing to do with the way Andi's breasts were so close to my chest the other night. Or the smell of her, soft and feminine. Innocent but uncompromising. She didn't need me to save her from the world, or from my teammates.

Why did I still want to? There was nothing rational about it. What she did and who she did it with, were none of my business, but if any of them touched her, I'd rip their arms off.

"Let's go." Flynn pushed himself up from his chair and nodded to Andi as he walked past. "Flynn Weston, it's nice to meet you. You might be just what the team needs. If any of the guys give you hell, let me know. I'm the team captain, and us redheads have to stick together." He ran a hand back and forth over his bright red buzz cut and smiled.

"I'll keep that in mind." Andi smiled back. "Thank you, Flynn." She blew out the side of her mouth to push a few strands of unruly curls aside. They flopped back the moment she stopped.

Blake all but shoved Nate out the door in front of me, a goofy grin on his face as he walked past her. Nate kept glancing back, his gaze dropping to the region of her ass.

They left me to follow behind slowly. I should walk right past her and not give her another glance, but I couldn't seem to control my own feet. Great, first my balls and cock rebel, now my legs. At least my brain was still working. More or less.

My treacherous feet stopped beside her. I took a moment to inhale her scent again. A hint of lavender mixed in with shampoo and something else. Possibly roses. Whatever it was, it smelled incredible.

My voice pitched low, I said, "About the other night."

"Message received, loud and clear," she said coolly. "Don't worry I won't offer you a...drink again." She looked at me expectantly.

It took me at least half a minute to realize what she was waiting for. "Cam," I said. "Cameron North. Left-winger. That's—"

"I know what a winger is, Mr. North," she said. "I suggest you focus on doing your job and leave me to do mine." She looked weary, like the last thing she wanted to do was have an argument with me. Or anyone else, for that matter.

Was she up to this job? If she wasn't, no doubt she'd find someone to palm it off onto. Someone who cared less about the team than she did. I got the impression she was at least trying. That, somehow, this landed in her lap at the last moment.

I added that to the ever-growing list of things that were not my problem. I should start writing them down and burning them, like my sister would have suggested I do. Or flushing them down the toilet. I didn't think paper was good for the sewerage system, so maybe I'd tear the paper up and throw it in the trash instead.

Either way, I needed to stop taking other people's problems on board.

"Of course, Ms. Welling." If she was going to

play it that way, then I'd roll with it. "Welcome to the Sea Dragons."

I gave her a curt nod before stepping past and out into the corridor. I'd like to put the other night firmly behind me, but I had a feeling it wasn't going to be forgotten so easily.

As long as she didn't let it get in the way of my career, then I'd shove it into the back of my mind and hope it stayed there.

Chapter Five

Andi

"For real?" Pia perched on a beanbag I was sure I didn't own this morning. Her face was pink with the effort of trying not to laugh.

"The guy who was an asshole to you the other night was Cam North? *The* Cam North? The Sea Dragons' forward?"

"Apparently." I opened a bottle of Chardonnay and poured us both a glass. "I had no idea who he was."

"You had no idea who any of them were until I insisted you look them up last night." She accepted the glass I handed her and took a sip. "If you told me what happened on Friday night, I would have insisted you point him out in the crowd."

I shrugged and downed a large gulp. "And then you would have confronted him."

"Of *course* I would have. No one messes with my sister and gets away with it." She set her drink down on the table in front of her and placed her hands in her lap. "Even if that means confronting Cameron North in public." She fanned herself with the tips of her fingers.

For some reason, that irritated me. Okay, he was attractive, with those dark eyes and biceps that looked like they were trying mercilessly to burst the seams of his T-shirt. But after the way he spoke to me, I wouldn't have offered him another... Drink anyway.

My clit might have sulked at that thought.

"What is his problem anyway?" I lowered myself onto the couch beside her and crossed my jean clad legs.

The moment I got home, I kicked off my heels and changed out of my skirt. I'd probably do some more work later, but I could *look* like I was in relaxation mode. Admittedly, it wasn't a mode I was familiar with. Even if I wasn't working, my brain was always going. I'd be lucky to spend a night without dreaming about work.

Yeah, maybe I was the one with the problem

here, but I was happy to let the focus be on him instead. Anything to keep my sister from teasing me, and trying to get me to run away to a deserted island with her. Or whatever her latest scheme was.

It was always something. Like her relationships with men, she flitted from one to the other. Photography seemed to be the only thing that had any permanency in her existence. That and her relationship with me. She dealt with our parents when she had to, always with a smile, never letting them get to her.

"Apart from being so hot it's a miracle the ice doesn't melt under his skates?" Pia asked.

"Apart from that," I said. "If he's such a big deal, why didn't you insist on me googling him last night?" That might have saved me looking like a stunned fish when I first saw him. She hadn't mentioned him. Not specifically anyway. Now I thought about it, I couldn't remember seeing anything about him apart from his name and stats.

"As far as I can tell, he has no social media accounts," she said. "The only time he appears in photos online, he's at the back, scowling like he doesn't want to be included in a team photo. Some guys are like that. They don't want the world all up in their business. Ironically, his sister Alice is a social media manager."

I understood why people didn't want to let social media into their lives. Guys like him were put under the microscope, every word they said analyzed for meaning and double meaning. I came under the same scrutiny from time to time. It was tedious, to say the least. Especially when people seemed more interested in my weight, than my accomplishments.

"He wasn't very friendly in person either," I said. "I guess he assumed I was interested in advancing my social media influence by spending time with him."

"My sister, the puck bunny." Pia grinned.

I made a face at her. "Says the one who wanted to go to Shells in the first place. Did you know they'd be there?"

"I might have," she admitted. "When you told me about Dad giving you the team—which is wild as hell, by the way—I thought it might be a good introduction. You could see them in their semi-native habitat. The ice being their native habitat."

I couldn't argue with that assessment. At the end of the arena tour, I'd spent some time watching the guys train. They all flew around the ice like they were born with skates on their feet.

If I tried that, I'd fall on my fluffy ass. Nothing and no one was getting me into a pair of ice skates. I'd sooner wear a bikini and walk down Lowball Bay's main beach.

Honestly, that was a lot more appealing. I could own the fact I had perfect breasts.

"Why do I get the impression you're more in touch with the nightlife of Lowball Bay than I am?" I took another sip of wine. It helped take the edge off the stress of the day.

"Because you never go out," she said. "Not unless I come down here and drag you out. I'm starting to think I should extend this visit to make sure you actually do some living for a change."

"I fit lots of living into my day," I protested. "I watered Laverne this morning."

Pia laughed. She went on laughing until she tipped backwards, falling off the beanbag and onto the floor. Her wine went with her, splashing Chardonnay down the front of her sweater.

"I think it's time to call last drinks for you," I said once I made sure she hadn't hurt herself on the hardwood floor.

She giggled and placed her empty glass on the table before gripping the hem of her sweater and shaking it in an attempt to make it dry. "I'm not drunk, just amused at your claim to have a life. You know what, it's a shame Cam North didn't take you up on that drink offer. I bet he knows how to show a girl a good time. He could have been exactly what you needed to kickstart you into a whole new vibe."

"I'm not sure I want to be kickstarted into anything," I said. "What's wrong with my life? I keep busy. My orchid is healthy. I'm sitting here drinking wine with my crazy baby sister."

"None of those things involve orgasms," Pia pointed out. "If you tell me there's more to life than orgasms, I'm going to fall off this beanbag again. And if you actually believe that, you really need to find a guy who can show you how things should be."

"How did we end up talking about orgasms?" I asked into my wine glass.

"Because, as your crazy baby sister, it's my job to point out that you need some." She nodded her head. "And I don't mean self-made ones. Those are good in the short term, don't get me wrong, but in the long term you need a man who will worship you for the beautiful goddess you are." She reached for the bottle to refill her glass.

"You might be overselling me a little bit, but I appreciate you, and what you're trying to say," I said. I tucked a curl behind my ear, but it bounced right back out again. "Don't you think I should take some time to move on from Xander first?"

"Xander Shmander." She waved her hand dismissively. "You know what they say. The best way to get over a guy is to get under another one. Especially a hot one like Cameron North."

"Nate Southwell seemed interested," I said slowly. "But it doesn't matter, because technically he works for me."

"Which brings us back to the proverbial elephant in the room," Pia said. "What did you do to have Dad punish you with extra work?" When I gave her a funny look, she elaborated. "He gave you an ice hockey team. The only thing he's ever given me is a stern look, like he thought I was wasting my life. And a top-of-the-line, state-of-the-art camera to get me started. But that was only because you insisted he give me something so I wouldn't set up a table in the center of Highball Creek, advising people on how to play the stock market based on a tarot reading."

She paused before admitting, "I do that too. It's a profitable side hustle, and very accurate. If you want, I'll do a reading for you. You could invest your millions and become a billionaire by the end of the year. Then you could stop working for Dad and chase your own dreams."

That was a lot to process.

"First of all, I like working for him," I said. "Second of all, I don't need to be a billionaire. If I made that much money, I'd give most of it away." I already gave sizable charitable donations to various causes. Anonymously, of course. I didn't need the credit for doing something people in my position should do because it was the right thing.

"Lastly, you know Dad, he likes to push us to be the best versions of ourselves. The team is his way of giving me something to challenge myself with."

"It's a test," she concluded. "To see if you can turn an okay team into an amazing team. Of course he wouldn't have done it out of the goodness of his heart. He tried that once with me, you know? He actually bought a hotel in Highball Creek and expected me to run it."

"You would have been amazing at it," I said.

"Of course I would, but I couldn't do it because he insisted on it," she said. "I gave the hotel to a friend of mine, Amelia. She'll do much better with it than I ever could. Maybe you should do that," she added brightly. "Give the team to someone. Dad didn't say you have to run it, did he?"

"It was implied," I said on a sigh.

He was used to Pia doing things like that, but I

could imagine what he'd say if I gave away an NHL team. I'd be lucky if he didn't fire me on the spot, and cut me off without a penny. "I want to run the team."

I needed a hasty gulp of wine before I continued with another admission. "I feel like my whole life has stagnated. Xander was a symptom of that. I need something new, something I can get my teeth into."

"Cameron North's ass?" Pia suggested with a grin.

I should totally not be picturing his naked ass right now. From what I'd seen of it, in denim and track pants, it was too firm to bite, but not too firm to lick.

My clit pulsed at the thought. I told it, and the image in my brain, to settle down and be quiet. There was no way in the world I was going to see Cam North's ass, much less lick it.

"You're thinking dirty thoughts about Cam North, aren't you?" Pia teased.

My face heated. "Of course not," I protested. "Like I said, he works for me. He's also made it clear he's not interested in me, even if I was interested in him. Which I'm not."

My clit would have said otherwise, but I ignored the throbbing.

"Sure." Pia drew out the word while rolling her

eyes toward the ceiling. "If the opportunity arises, I dare you to take it."

"It won't," I assured her. He and I were going to be completely professional from here on out. Boss and hot ice hockey player, nothing more.

"In the meantime." I fixed her with my best stern big sister look, which would probably have her laughing hard enough to fall off the beanbag again, if I wasn't careful. "We need to talk about you giving away a hotel."

Chapter Six

Cam

"Okay, spill." Nate stopped in front of the
treadmill and draped himself over the display. He
looked up at and watched me run, his head cocked,
one eyebrow raised.

"Spill is not a good word to use for a guy that's on
a treadmill," Blake remarked. He was running on the
one beside me, face glistening with sweat.

If I pretended I couldn't hear either of them
because of the earbuds in my ears, how long would it
take for Nate to go away? With frustration, I realized
it was too long. I pulled out my right earbud and held
it in my fist.

"What?" I snapped. It was only a matter of time
before he approached me, wanting the gossip. I was
surprised it took until now.

"You and Andi," he said, smirking at my obvious discomfort.

"What about us?" I asked. There was no 'us,' I knew that much.

"When she turned up at the meeting yesterday, you and her seemed to know each other. Judging by the way you bristled after I suggested giving her a tour, you know each other pretty well." He straightened his head, but the expectant expression on his face remained.

"I did not bristle," I said. "I don't give a crap what you and her do. It's nothing to do with me." I started to put my earbud back in.

"Sorry, Cam, but you definitely bristled," Blake said. "Was it just because she knew who I was and not you?"

I glanced over at him without breaking stride. "I don't give a shit about that. Since when do I care about being recognized?"

"Never before now," Blake agreed. "There's a first time for everything."

I smirked and turned away. "We might have met when we were at Shells the other night."

Nate grinned. "Did you hook up with the boss? Way to go, Cam." He offered me a fist bump, which I ignored.

"I did not hook up with her," I said. I pressed a couple of buttons on the display to slow the treadmill to a walk. "We literally bumped into each other. She offered me a drink. I said no."

"You turned her down?" Nate frowned. "No offense, bro, but you need your eyes checked. She's adorable." He was clearly trying to provoke a response from me.

I wasn't going to give him one. Not in the way he wanted.

"Yes, I turned her down," I said, my voice tight. "I told her I don't fuck puck bunnies."

I remembered the look in her eyes when I said that, right before I pushed off the wall and stomped away like a dickhead. She had no idea what provoked me to respond that way, and now I knew why. Until yesterday, she didn't have a clue who I was. If I had to guess, I'd suggest she knew very little about hockey. She probably cared even less.

Nate stared at me for a moment, then grinned. "You thought Andi Welling was a puck bunny? That's absolute gold."

I shook my head. "Who is she anyway?"

"You didn't look her up?" Blake also slowed to a walk. Now, he reached into the pocket of his shorts to pull out his phone and point the screen towards me.

I peered at it for a moment before grabbing the phone and holding it up. "Andrea Welling, daughter of billionaire property developer Harrison Welling. Executive at Welling Developments. Approximate net worth..." My eyes almost bugged out of my head. The article was accompanied by a photo of her in business wear, standing beside an older man in a suit. Her father, I presumed.

I handed the phone back to Blake and continued walking. "So what? She's some spoiled little rich girl who somehow now owns our team."

"I think it's safe to say she's not a puck bunny," Nate said. "It wouldn't surprise me if she knew exactly who all of us were. She might have turned up that night to feel us out. And you had the chance to feel her out, literally, but you turned her down." He clicked his tongue.

"If that's the kind of person she is, I dodged a bullet," I said.

If she'd sneak around, pretending to be someone she wasn't, then she wasn't the sort of woman I was interested in. Instinct told me she wasn't like that, but it might have been my balls, which were bluer by the day.

"I would have gone there," Zack called out from one of the stationary bikes. "The chick has money and a pussy, what more does anyone need?"

Without thinking, I threw my earbud at him, hitting him in the side of the face.

"What the hell?" he protested.

"She's the boss, have some respect." I glared at him until he looked away.

"Is that all she is?" Nate asked. "Because if she's not, you won't mind if I ask her out."

I wanted to pull out my other earbud and throw it at him. "Like you said, she's not a puck bunny. Women like that want more than a one night stand. Since we all know you can't and won't give her more than that, I suggest you save it for the girls who only want some fun."

I thought he might argue with me, just because he could, but instead he nodded.

"You're right," he admitted. "She does seem like the commitment type." He grimaced, before it slowly became a grin. "Seems more like your type than mine."

If she was anyone else in the world, maybe. She was gorgeous and intelligent. But she'd turned up at Shells, behaving all innocent, when she clearly wasn't. She pretended she didn't know who I was, which wasn't something a person didn't do unless they had an agenda.

With people like her and her father, it was usually one thing—money. If her goal was to improve the team performance this season, then sell the Sea Dragons at a profit, the sooner she was gone, the better.

If nothing else, it was a good incentive to stay at the top of my game. We'd win, and then we'd be rid of her.

I ignored my balls' suggestion that they didn't want to be rid of her. Sneaky, and with an ulterior motive wasn't sexy, but my balls insisted it was.

"Who is Cam's type?" Flynn wiped his face with a towel and stepped over to us. He'd been in the corner, lifting weights and listening to what was probably an audiobook. Whenever he was listening to those, he got that engrossed look on his face, like the rest of the world disappeared and he was lost in the story. Even Nate couldn't budge him out of it.

"Andi Welling," Nate said, clearly enjoying being the bearer of gossip. He briefly told Flynn about the rest of our conversation, while I went on walking and trying to ignore them both.

"You really think she pretended she had no idea who you were?" Flynn asked me.

I shrugged. "Makes sense. She knew who Blake was, but only admitted when Zack started being a dick. She wanted to shoot him down."

Zack gave me the side eye, but went on cycling. "I'd still go there."

"I don't think she'd *want* you to go there," Blake called out to him. "She has better taste than that."

Any woman with a brain cell or two to rub together had more sense than to go for a player like Zack. According to some of the guys, he had mirrors in his bedroom so he could watch himself with whichever puck bunny he could convince to go home with him.

I didn't know if that was true, but I wouldn't have been surprised to learn it was. I kept the visual image out of my brain before I needed to invest in a factory to make brain bleach. Zack Reed naked was the last thing I wanted to picture.

Because you want to picture Andi, my subconscious whispered. *Here's one of her crawling towards you on your bed.*

I shoved the image back into a corner of my mind for later, when I was alone. The arena gym was top of my list of places I didn't want to get hard. Hard body yes, hard cock no.

Zack gave Blake a look to suggest he'd convince

her otherwise given half a chance. He turned away, ducked his head and cycled faster.

I pressed the treadmill display to turn it off and walked until it came to a stop. "I don't know what her game is. I don't know what she wants with the team, or any of us. All I know is the only game I play is ice hockey. I don't play games with women and I don't play games with the team's owner. If that's her jam, I don't want anything to do with it. I'm here to do my job and do it well. If she tries to screw with that, we'll deal with her. Right now, let's focus on what matters: winning."

I grabbed the towel, which hung over the side of the treadmill, and hid my frustrated expression behind the cotton, wiping the sweat from my face.

"Sounds like a good game plan," Flynn agreed. "She might be just what we need."

I lowered the towel just enough to reveal my eyes so he could see me stare at him.

"Ome un ohh as..." I pulled the towel away from my mouth so I could speak more clearly. "Someone who has no interest in the team? Whose knowledge of hockey either consists of googling some of us the night before she met us, or googling us all and pretending she didn't? How is that what we need?"

Whichever of those options was the truth, they

were both the opposite of what we needed. Even if she was wrapped up in a sexy package with hair I wanted to wrap my fist around. Those plush lips would look perfect sucking on my...

Shit, I needed to stop thinking this way. Nothing was ever going to happen between me and Andi Welling.

"We can teach her," Flynn said easily. "She said she's not going to make big changes. Would you prefer someone coming in and tearing everything down to start over? Someone who thinks they know everything and doesn't want to hear what we have to say? I know you don't. I think we can work with her." He gave me a speculative look.

I looked back at him before I realized what he wasn't saying. "You think *I* should work with her?"

"Why not you?" he asked. "You're direct with people. Usually," he added when Nate started to speak. "You won't try to get into her pants the way Nate will."

"Guilty." Nate grinned.

"You won't piss her off the way Zack will," Blake said, getting in on the pile-on.

"And it would give you the opportunity to make up for making assumptions about her on the night you met," Flynn concluded.

"What if I talk to her and find out my assumptions are right?" I asked.

"You're the best man to do that," Blake said. "People like to tell you the truth. They know you're a straight shooter. If she was pretending, you're our best chance of finding out."

"Blake is right," Flynn said. "People open up to you."

"People fill the awkward silence," I muttered. I doubted it was because they thought I was a good listener. I made them so uncomfortable they felt the need to say something.

I glanced around, but it didn't look like any of them was going to back down. "Fine, I'll apologize to her for being an asshat. But that's all. There's no reason for me to spend time with her after that. I'll apologize because it's the respectful thing to do. But for the record, she'll probably tell me to get lost."

I hoped she would. That would give me even more reason to stay the hell away from her.

It was going to be a long season.

Chapter Seven

Andi

"Oh em gee." Rafe looked around himself as he stepped into the office.

At some point, I might start to think of it as mine, but I hadn't yet. Especially not with the space decorated the way it currently was.

The desk was huge, made of heavy, dark wood. It reminded me of the one in my father's office. The chairs and leather couch were a match, screaming masculinity and power. There was nothing wrong with furniture saying either of those things, but they weren't to my taste.

I preferred not to be in people's faces like this. Or worse, make people uncomfortable the moment they stepped through the door.

My father would have sat behind the desk and

looked down his nose at anyone on the other side, reminding them who was in charge here. I couldn't even bring myself to sit in the chair behind it. The couch was more comfortable. It was located in front of a window with a gorgeous view of Lowball Bay.

To be fair, so was the desk, but I preferred a more casual approach.

If my father could see me now, he'd lose his mind. That was fine. He did things his way and I did them mine. As far as I was concerned, life was too short to let everyone assume your head was buried up your ass.

"This is ah-mazing," Rafe said. He placed his backpack down beside the couch and flopped down hard enough to bounce a couple of times. "It's about time we had a corner office."

"We?" I opened my water bottle and took a sip.

"Of course, we," he said with no hint of apology. "We're a team. Otherwise, I'd be back at Welling, trying to figure out what coffee your replacement prefers." He wrinkled his nose. "Instead, we're here, home of the hottest hockey players in the hemisphere." In a loud whisper, he said, "Are any of them gay?"

I clicked my tongue at him. "You're married."

He sniffed and crossed his legs at his knees. "Of

course I am, but I'm not dead. Jacoby doesn't mind me looking."

"If you're only looking, then what does it matter if they're gay?" I snatched up a handful of notes from the table in front of us and started to skim them. I'd asked Coach Lampton to give me his thoughts on the best places to spend money to improve the team.

Evidently, he had lots of thoughts. Most pertaining to the replacement of equipment that should have been retired a year or two ago. I couldn't argue with any of those suggestions. After all, he was the expert here.

Rafe shrugged and peered over my shoulder. "If you told me a couple of weeks ago Andi Welling was taking on a hockey team, I would have laughed my ass off."

"Me too," I said. "I admit I'm scared I might be over my head."

I wouldn't have said that to another person, but I trusted my assistant more than I trusted anyone else.

In the three years we'd been working together, he always had my back. And he wasn't afraid to call me out if I needed it. If he agreed with something I said, I knew he meant it.

"Because of the job, or because of the hot hockey players?" he asked.

"Both," I said. "Some of them...don't seem to want me here."

One particular name sprang to mind. Cam North would probably be ecstatic if I found a replacement, packed up and left.

Too bad for him. Even if I had nothing to prove to my father, Cam wanting me out was a fantastic reason to stay. I'd dealt with enough men like that in the past that I wasn't intimidated by him now.

Memories of his body so close to mine in Shells, then the expression on his face when he saw me step into that meeting, were both seared into my brain, for different reasons. I reminded myself I couldn't let him get under my skin. He was a grumpy, professional hockey player who worked for me. That was all.

"I'm going to drop that straight in the 'too fucking bad' bucket," Rafe said, flicking back dark hair that fell over his eye. "Our girl is here now, in charge of this whole shebang." He spread his hands to gesture around the office. "And we both know you're going to kill it. I know you, it won't take long for you to convince them of that. And if they don't like it, I'm sure you could organize a transfer to somewhere that will welcome their asses. Toronto is nice and cold this time of year." He punctuated his words with a wicked smile.

"I don't think disliking the team owner is grounds for transferring a player," I said. "I have a funny feeling that would create more problems than it would solve. Anyway," I shook my head. "I don't care if they like me or not, as long as they're loyal to their team and teammates."

Rafe snorted as loud as one of the geese that ran wild in Highball Creek. "You can say you don't care as much as you want, but I know you better than that. You like to be liked. Or at least, you don't like to be *disliked*." He frowned at his own words, as if unsure if he had them straight. Finally, he decided he had and nodded once.

"No one likes to be disliked," I said. "For the record, I don't need to be liked, but I do like to be respected." Whether it was working directly for my father, or doing this, I put everything into it, so I could earn people's respect. Even if I sacrificed relationships, like the one with Xander.

Were my priorities mixed up? I liked to think they weren't. Respect was important. Difficult to gain and ridiculously easy to lose.

"I respect you," Rafe said. "Why a hockey team? A football team would have been just as much fun. I love the Humpbacks! Or you know what would have been great?" He was all but bouncing up and down in his seat. "Pickleball. I can see it now." He raised a hand in front of him to sketch the image in the air. "The Lowball Bay Nudibranch Pickleball Team."

I laughed. "Nudibranch?"

"Yep. They're a kind of sea slug, but with a much better name. As an added bonus, it goes with the Sea Dragons, Starfish, Humpbacks and the Sea Cucumbers. All of the male professional athletes in the Bay are basically seamen." His expression was deadpan.

I laughed again. "Next thing you'll suggest is changing the name of the city to Seamen Bay."

"Now that would just be silly," Rafe sniffed, but his eyes shone with humor. "It would have to be Seamenball Bay."

I snorted a little too loudly. "I stand corrected. Whatever was I thinking?"

He grinned. "I was wondering that myself. Hey, imagine the pickleball team mascot. It could look like a sea bunny. Although, that might be more appropriate for a hockey team."

I appreciated the irony in that suggestion. "I'll bear that in mind if there's ever a professional pickleball team in Lowball Bay," I assured him. "It's not really a team sport though. In the meantime, what we have is an ice hockey team that's performing well, but on paper should be doing a lot better."

"According to whom?" Rafe asked.

"This." I tapped the sheets of paper against my knee. "And according to Coach Lambton. He actually offered me his resignation while he was showing me around the building. Which I declined, because I saw the way the team respected him at the meeting. If they didn't think he could take them to the next level, they wouldn't have been so relaxed and respectful."

"Not to mention if the head coach leaves right after you start here, people are going to suggest you fired his ass," Rafe said. "And that would be a great way to create tension and maybe bad blood."

"Unless they didn't like him," I said. "In which case, I'd be viewed more favorably. But they do and that's not a wave I'm going to make. According to my research, he's respected throughout the NHL. Several other teams were vying to have him take over as head coach over the last few seasons. He knows what he's doing."

I brushed a handful of curls off the side of my face and pressed my hand to my head to keep them back out of the way.

"But you wish you knew more about hockey," Rafe stated.

"Exactly," I agreed. "I'm trusting that people know how to do their jobs, but what if they don't? Did you ever have that teacher at school all the kids loved because they didn't make them work? I worry he's like that."

"First of all, I don't think I ever had a teacher like that," Rafe said slowly. "And second, you don't think that about him, do you? You're a better judge of character than that. After all, you hired me out of all those applicants." He shifted from side to side as though he was somehow bashful.

"I can't decide if you're making your point or not," I teased. When he playfully pouted, I smiled. "I'm glad I hired you. I was getting tired of the people who agreed with me no matter what. What's the point of surrounding yourself with people like that?"

"Only you would ask that question," Rafe said. "Some people like people like that. People who won't argue with them or tell them they're wrong. Then they get to feel right all the time."

I grimaced. "That's so wrong. Not to mention unhealthy. And unproductive too. If I had people like that around me, I'd spend half my time fixing up mistakes I didn't realize I was making."

"Yes, you would," he said. "You *should* blame them and make them clean them up." He didn't add, 'like your father would.' The words hung between us.

My father and I couldn't have had more different approaches to just about everything. Sometimes I wondered why I wanted to work for him, but the answer was simple. I wanted to learn from him so I could take over and do his job better than he did.

If we had anything in common, it was ambition. Something I suspected Xander never fully understood or appreciated. He would have been happy if I stopped working and had babies instead.

Someday, I wanted children, but for now I had other priorities. Not to mention if I couldn't keep an orchid alive, I had no business having a baby. Apparently babies needed more than water every few days.

"I'll get us some coffee and you can talk me through your plan," Rafe said. He placed his hands to either side of him on the leather couch and pushed himself to his feet. He stepped out from behind the table and stopped.

"Looks like we have company," he said.

I knew that tone, it hinted at a warning for me, as well as the new arrival.

Rafe had always been somewhat protective of

me, even when I insisted I didn't need him to be. He would happily have kicked, or kneed, someone in the balls if absolutely necessary.

It was sweet, but I could handle myself. Most of the time.

I didn't need him to tell me we weren't alone either. Even before Rafe said the words, I felt the air leave the huge room. The temperature shot up several notches.

I tried to ignore the sweat that broke out on my palms before I looked over and saw the big winger standing beside the door-frame, looking uncomfortable.

"Mr. North."

Chapter Eight

Cam

I rubbed a hand over the back of my neck and met the eye of the slender man who looked at me like I was an oversized dog and he was a Chihuahua. He was smaller than me, but his posture suggested he knew how to bite if necessary. He held my gaze, giving me a silent warning before he brushed past and swept out of the office.

"Ms. Welling." I dropped my hand down to my side with a slap of skin on denim. I tried not to look at her too hard, but I couldn't tear my eyes away.

She looked at home on that black leather couch. Her sweater today was emerald green. The shade made her hair look redder, and her eyes deeper blue. She wore very little make-up, leaving her freckles to decorate the pale skin of her heart-shaped face.

Her lips were pressed in a line as she looked back at me. Not hostile, but not welcoming either. I didn't miss the way her eyes dipped down below the waistband of my worn jeans. Her cheeks turned slightly pink before her gaze snapped back to my face.

"Did you want something?" she asked coolly.

You, lying back on that couch, writhing underneath me while I...

I cleared my throat and shoved the thought away. "I came to apologize. For the other night."

"Okay," she said simply. Her expression gave me little to work with. Was she accepting my apology or waiting for more?

"I was aggressive and out of line," I continued. Now I was the one filling the awkward silence.

She nodded finally. "You *were* aggressive and out of line. Would you be apologizing if I didn't own your team?"

"If you didn't, chances are I'd never see you again," I pointed out. "Can't apologize to someone if you have no idea who they are."

"I suppose that's true," she conceded. "If you never saw me again, would you be sorry for what you did? Or are you only sorry because of who I turned out to be?"

"Does it matter?" I asked. She wasn't making this

apology easy. When I pictured in my mind how this would go, it was to give her a quick 'sorry,' and step back out of the office. I'd have this off my chest and wouldn't have to deal with her, except from a distance.

"I think it does," she said. "There's a difference between saying sorry because you want to and saying sorry because you feel you have to. If I was some random woman you never saw again, would you have given it a second thought?"

I pressed my teeth together and rolled my lips a couple of times. "Probably not."

"So you talk that way to women on a regular basis?" she asked.

I stared at her for a moment. "No. Yes. I don't... Fuck." I scrubbed a hand over the stubble on my chin. "I usually keep my distance. I don't go around running into women."

"Just me," she said.

"Technically, you ran into me," I pointed out. "Do you run into men and offer them a drink on a regular basis?"

"Just you," she said. "But running into you was an accident. The offer of a drink was my way of making up for being a klutz."

"So you want me to take you for a drink before

you'll accept my apology?" That idea was more appealing than it should have been. I should turn and get the hell out of here right now.

"That wasn't what I was saying, but that's not a bad idea," she said. "We got off on the wrong foot. Maybe we could try again. We might get off on the right foot this time."

If she kept using the expression 'get off,' we were going to have a problem, in the form of a boner in the front of my jeans. Okay, that was more of a problem for me than it was for her, but she was going to witness it in all its blood-engorged glory.

"Do you know anything about hockey?" I blurted out. I cocked my head at her and silently dared her to admit the limit to her knowledge. She'd tied me in knots, it was time to return the favor.

She sighed and tossed a handful of papers onto the table in front of her. They slid across the surface and floated to the floor on the other side.

"I meant what I said in that meeting room. I googled a couple of you the night before, over wine with my sister. From what she's told me, I wouldn't have found much about you anyway."

Now she was daring me to admit— What? That I hated social media with a burning passion? When it came to things I never wanted to deal with, it was right up there with having warts all over my dick. For the record, no, I never had warts on my dick.

I shrugged. "I don't feel the need to share my life with the world. It makes less trouble for the PR team. They don't have to worry about me posting photos of that night's puck bunny and having them go viral." Compared to that, dick warts didn't sound so bad.

"Is that why you stay away from them?" she asked. "Because they want the publicity that might come from being associated with you?"

She hit the nail way too close to the head for my liking.

"Something like that," I agreed. I pressed my lips together, hoping she'd get the hint that I didn't want to talk about it. "The guys think I should teach you about ice hockey."

"Do they?" She stood and walked around the table before crouching down to pick the sheets of paper up off the floor.

My balls were quick to point out that her face was now at just the right height. I could almost feel her lips wrapped around me. Her tongue teasing me, cheeks inward as she sucked.

Shit. *Quick, come up with some coherent response before she thinks you're a complete idiot.*

"Yep."

That was more or less coherent. Go me. Yeah, sometimes I was my own cheerleader for the most dumbass reasons. Someone had to be.

"And what do you think?" She glanced up at me before tapping the edge of the papers on the edge of the table to line them all up.

"I figure, if we're getting a drink anyway," I said slowly. "I could give you a few pointers."

Yes please, my cock replied. *I know exactly where to point.*

Shut up, I told it. *She's the boss, remember?* She was also way too cute for my own good and probably hers. Was it too late to withdraw the offer of a drink, and teaching her about the game?

"You know what, maybe it's a bad idea," I said. I took a couple of steps back, until I ran into the door frame.

Very smooth, I told myself.

"Maybe it is." She placed a hand on the table and pushed herself to her feet. "Who would you suggest then? Nate? Zack? Or maybe Blake? They all seem nice enough."

"No," I said a bit too quickly. When she raised an eyebrow, I knew she had me well and truly trapped, and not just against the side of the door. How had I gotten myself into this position?

"No?" she echoed.

"Nate is a player," I said. "He thinks with the stick in his pants more than he does with one in his hand. I mean, the one for playing hockey, not... You know."

She smiled at that, showing that one crooked tooth with all the perfect ones. The expression reached her eyes, brightening the room more than the sunlight that poured through the window.

"And the other two?" she prompted.

Her smile had faded too quickly. I wanted to see it again.

"Zack has mirrors in his bedroom," I blurted. "He looks into them and asks who's the hottest player of all." I had no idea if he actually did, but I was rewarded with a peal of laughter that sent a jolt of heat all the way through me. Even my cold, dead heart beat a little faster.

"And what about Blake?" She looked expectant, amused.

How was I supposed to top that?

I shrugged. "Blake lives at home. I don't know, but he probably sleeps in those pajamas with the feet attached." I pointed down to my worn sneakers.

That drew another laugh from between her

pillowy lips. "Maybe I like a guy who sleeps in footie pajamas."

"You seem more like the type who likes a guy who doesn't sleep in pajamas at all," I said without thinking.

"Like you?" Her gaze dropped below the waistband of my jeans again. Her cheeks turned flaming red. She looked back at my face, eyes wide, hand pressed to her chest, right over her luscious cleavage.

"I'm sorry. Now I'm the one who's out of line. I didn't mean to—"

I pushed myself off the door frame and took a couple of steps towards her, my hand stretched out, palm raised toward her. "It's okay. I went there first. No harm, no foul."

"Right," she said uneasily. She swallowed hard. If I didn't know better, I'd think she was picturing me naked. And liking what she saw.

I should retreat back behind the red line. Get safely into my defensive zone and stay there. I should have come here with padding and a helmet on, stick in hand, to keep a safe distance from her. To keep her a safe distance from me.

Who was I kidding? She was better off on the other side of the city from me, not in the same room.

"So, about giving me pointers about hockey," she said in a rush.

"My place," we said at the same time.

That was followed by both of us saying, "Your place."

Shit, could this get any more awkward?

"Shells?" I suggested.

"People will talk," she replied. "If you like to keep your life private, that would be a bad idea."

"For both of us," I agreed.

"Right," she said awkwardly. "We don't want people to assume there's anything going on between us when there's not."

"No, there isn't," I said. "If there was, I wouldn't want people to talk about us."

"Would you be ashamed of having a relationship with me?" Why did that seem to bother her so much? What almost seemed like hurt flashed through her blue eyes. Unless I imagined it. Yeah, of course I did. That made sense. No way would she be hurt by that for real. Probably.

"No, 'course not," I said. "But nothing is going to happen between us, so let's not give anyone the wrong impression. Right?"

"Right." She blinked a couple of times. "Right."

She stepped over to the oversized desk and opened a couple of drawers before she found some paper and a pen. She wrote something on a sheet and folded it over before handing it to me. "My address and phone number. I trust you won't share this with anyone else. Especially guys who sleep in pajamas with feet." She managed a watery smile. "You know where that is?"

I unfolded the paper and glanced at her flowery, but neat writing. "I can find the place." Yeah, I knew the address. It was close to my apartment. Close enough that I could walk.

Not far for a booty call, my cock hinted.

Okay, that might have been the back of my brain. Apparently only the rational part of my mind was still keeping its pants on.

"Great. I'll line up a couple of replays and you can talk me through it." Her tongue swiped over her plump lower lip.

I managed to tear my eyes away from her mouth and tuck the paper into the back pocket of my jeans. "I'll bring dinner."

And no pajamas, I silently added. Not just because I slept naked, but because this was one thousand percent not a date. I'd explain a few things, then leave. I wouldn't even take a moment to look back. No way.

Now, if I could just convince the rest of myself of that.

Chapter Nine

Andi

"You invited Cam North to your place?" Pia practically shrieked down the line, right into my ear.

"It's not a big deal," I told her.

"Suuure," she said with a laugh. "You called me to tell me it's no big deal?"

"It really isn't," I insisted. She was right though, I did call her. She'd headed back to Highball Creek that morning. I missed her already, in spite of her apparent attempt to permanently damage my hearing. I knew she'd read more into this, just like Rafe had. He'd tried to give me advice on what to wear and what to say.

I reminded him several times it wasn't a date. He gave me a disbelieving look, but left it at that. For now. No doubt he'd want a blow by blow description of everything that happened tonight.

Which would definitely not involve blowing.

"It's so he can teach me about hockey." I held up a sage green sweater in front of myself. After a brief, critical squint in the mirror, I shook my head and folded it carefully to place back on the shelf.

I rejected an emerald green sweater and a sapphire blue blouse before deciding on a long sleeved white blouse and jeans. The casual outfit was perfectly adequate for this non-date.

I shrugged into the perfectly pressed blouse and adjusted the phone against my ear while I did up the buttons.

"What's to learn?" she asked. "If they hit the puck just right, it slides effortlessly across the smooth, smooth ice and right into the warm embrace of the goal."

"Can you not make hockey sound like sex?" I grimaced.

"It's not my fault a game that's played with big, long sticks is provocative," she said with a laugh. "It's not my fault you interpreted it that way either. Maybe your subconscious is reminding you how long it's been since you got laid. Otherwise, you would have heard something perfectly innocent."

"Bullshit," I replied. "There's nothing innocent about you or most of the stuff that comes out of your mouth. You're the one who horrifies our parents as often as you can, just for a giggle."

"Not true," she argued. "I say stuff and they take it the wrong way. Can I help it if they have dirty minds? That must be where you get it from."

I snorted. "If you're as innocent as you say you are, then I'm a yeti."

Pia laughed. "That would explain a lot. Especially your crazy hair and huge feet."

"I do not have huge feet!" I protested. I glanced down at them, just in case. Nope, perfectly normal, size seven feet.

Great, now I was remembering the conversation with Cam about pajamas with no feet. And the way I'd pictured him, with no pajamas, lying in the middle of my bed, cock jutting up invitingly. His brown eyes watching me move toward him, crawling across the mattress, my breasts heavy, body aching with need.

"Says you," Pia teased. "This is exactly how people get nicknames, Bigfoot."

"Shut up," I said while laughing, and trying desperately to get the visual image of the big forward out of my mind.

You're his boss, I reminded myself for the seventy billionth time. We made it clear this was not a date.

I was physically attracted to him, but he'd done nothing to suggest he liked me.

Why was he coming here then? He'd said the team thought he should be the one to explain the game to me. That was all it was. He was taking one for the team. Spending an hour or two of his time with the boss, so the Sea Dragons didn't look bad when anyone mentioned the game to me.

The team had a good point. Right now, my response to questions about hockey would be a blank look. Sure, I could spout out stats, and I could give anyone a decent rundown of the Sea Dragons' finances, but I couldn't tell if they played well or badly on any given night.

Was that the point of my father giving me the team? Was it possible he was hoping I'd screw up? That for some reason, he was waiting for me to fall on my face? Why, I didn't know. He didn't explain himself to anyone, much less to me.

"At least Bigfoot is more original than Red," Pia said. "Or Pea Soup." Some of the kids at school thought that was a hilarious nickname for her. Soup for short.

"Now I want some pea soup," I complained.

As hard as they tried, the nickname hadn't stuck. Mostly because Pia loved pea soup so much she used to bring a thermos of it to school. She embraced it, right up until they finally let up.

"Sorry, not sorry," she said. "I should have invested in a soup factory."

"You'd eat it all," I said. "Or is that, drink it all?" What was the correct terminology for the consumption of liquid food? Whatever it was, the product wouldn't make it to the shelves.

"I predict you finishing this call and ordering some soup," Pia said. "City slicker."

"Country bumpkin," I retorted. "For the record, Cam is bringing dinner."

"So it *is* a date?" She sounded like she was bouncing up and down on the other end of the call. "Go Andi! You might get laid after all."

"It is not a date," I said firmly. "I am not sleeping with Cameron North. Not today. Not ever."

"What if you sell the team?" she asked. "What if he retires from hockey and starts up a new job as a door to door soup salesman?"

I shook my head and laughed. "I don't think that's a thing. Even if it was, I know how much he gets paid. Unless he's blown it all, he doesn't need to go door to door selling anything."

"Andi said blown," Pia teased.

"Pia might be the one who needs to get laid," I said. "You seem to be seeing sex where there's no potential for it."

There was nothing between Cam and I but a brief physical attraction. If I took a moment and thought back to the way he spoke to me in Shells, that should make it easier to convince myself of that. But while he was right when he said he was aggressive that night, I hadn't hated it. He seemed like the kind of man who knew how to take control and give a girl more orgasms than she knew what to do with.

And if I kept thinking that way, I was going to ruin my panties.

"I should have stayed in town," Pia said. "If you don't want him—"

"You're not going there either," I said quickly.

Her words shouldn't have rubbed me the wrong way. It had nothing to do with my attraction to him. No way. It was just that...she shouldn't assume he was down for a fling with her either.

Just because she was smart, cute and guys always looked at her twice before they even noticed me, didn't mean he'd do the same.

A small voice in the back of my head said he absolutely would. What guy wouldn't go for a woman like my sister? She could snap her fingers and he'd follow her like a puppy.

For the first time since she left the city, I was almost glad she was gone. Why did I care though? Pia and Cam would be cute together. Didn't they deserve to be happy, if that was the choice they both made?

Why did a flare of envy ignite inside me? It was completely irrational. I had no claim to him. No reason to believe he thought of me as anything other than the owner of the team he played for. Someone who would embarrass the team if he didn't sit down with me and explain the game.

"You do like him," Pia said.

"No, I don't," I protested.

"Then why did you get all possessive just now?" she asked. "I could almost feel the daggers coming straight out of your eyeballs, headed right at the center of my forehead."

"You have a vivid imagination," I said. "There are no daggers. I was totally *not* being possessive."

"And denial is a river bun Egypt," she said. "There's nothing wrong with being attracted to someone. You're both adults. He's hot. You're adorable and smart. Admit it, you want to know how big his cock is."

"Pia!" I scolded. "I shouldn't be thinking about any of his body parts."

Yes, I wanted to know how big his cock was. Judging by the bulge in the front of his jeans, it was big. Big enough to fill me just right, while his toned body pressed me down onto the bed. While my fingernails grazed his muscular biceps.

"Now you're thinking about all of his body parts," she said gleefully. "Admit it to yourself, even if you won't admit it to me."

"There's nothing to admit," I protested. "Because it doesn't matter anyway. We're going to be professionals, behaving professionally."

"Over dinner that he's bringing," she said persistently.

"I'm starting to think I shouldn't have told you anything," I said.

"Of course you should have," she said. "If you don't tell me, who are you going to tell?"

"I have friends," I said.

"None whom you trust to tell them that he's coming over," she pointed out. "Is that because they'd judge you, or because you know they'd call you out if they looked you right in the face?"

I chose option C, both of the above.

"It's because they're busy," I argued. "And I

wanted to talk to my baby sister. A move I'm starting to regret."

Phone between my neck and my shoulder, I stepped into one leg of my jeans. I tried to step into the other leg, while keeping the phone from falling, but I couldn't hold the jeans in place and raise my foot high enough at the same time.

I took a breath and tried again. I got my foot inside the denim, but only half way down the leg. I tugged, trying to pull the fabric up and disentangle my foot at the same time. My toes got stuck somewhere near the hem.

All my weight on my right foot, I jumped up and down a couple of times and shook my leg, trying to push the left one through.

With a barely bitten back curse, I lost my balance. My hip hit the shelf beside me. I squeaked in pain and dropped my phone.

I tried to grab it with the hand that wasn't holding up my pants, but it slipped out of my grip. The device landed on the floor and bounced before stopping, screen down.

I shoved my foot all the way into the other leg and tugged my jeans over my hips before scooping my phone up and grimacing at the newest crack.

I put it back to my ear. "You still there?"

"Yeah, you good?"

"I'm fine." Mostly.

I stepped out of my bedroom and exhaled in the direction of my balcony. It was in darkness, but the city lights beyond that twinkled, like a thousand eyes winking at me and reading all of my inner secrets. Past that, the ocean was illuminated by a moon which would be full in a night or two. "What were we saying?"

"Something about you regretting calling me, but we both know you don't," she laughed. "You love talking to me. Because I'm honest with you when other people aren't. And right now, I'm going to be honest and say you have a crush. Even if you won't admit it. It is what it is."

I could almost see her nodding to punctuate the sentence. When she decided she was right about something, she was almost impossible to budge. She meant well, but her pushing wouldn't lead to anything. No matter how much she wanted to believe otherwise.

No matter how much *I* wanted to believe otherwise.

"It doesn't matter if I have a crush," I said. "I couldn't act on it anyway, even if he was interested, which he's not. So do me a favor and let it go. Find some nice guy so we can gossip about you next time."

"I don't think there are any nice guys in Highball Creek that are still single," she complained. "Except Lenny. Rumor has it, he likes to peep into women's windows when the drapes aren't drawn all the way across."

"He sounds like a catch," I said dryly.

"He's a catch for the cops," she replied. "Still, he's mostly harmless, in an I'm-not-going-there kind of way. I mean, he's close to eighty years old."

"Just think how experienced he'd be," I deadpanned.

She responded with a gagging sound. "I'll give you his number," she said. "You two could be cute together. There wouldn't be any issue with you being his boss. And you wouldn't have to worry about him biting, because he has no teeth."

"That's very kind of you, but I wouldn't want to get between you and your true love," I teased. Of all the things people might say about Cam North, I was almost certain he wasn't a peeping Tom. He seemed more like the kind of man who'd tear the drapes down, not peek between them.

"Don't let me get between you and yours," Pia

said. "Enjoy your night with Cam. I want to hear all the juicy details later."

Before I could respond, she said goodbye and ended the call.

Not two minutes later, a knock sounded on my front door.

Cue a wave of nervous excitement. I tried to push it aside, but it persisted all the way across the room, until I opened the door.

"Hey."

Chapter Ten

Cam

"Hey."

I stepped inside her apartment and handed her the warm paper bag of food I'd just picked up from my favorite restaurant around the corner. "I hope you like Chinese. The Golden Duck has the best wonton soup and spring rolls in the city."

She pressed her lips together and smiled as though she was trying to hold back a laugh. "I love Chinese." She carried the bag over to the kitchen and unfolded the top.

Steam rose into the air, filling the space with the scent of ginger, garlic and spices.

"That smells amazing." She half-closed her eyes and inhaled.

I bet the food didn't smell as good as her.

She pulled the containers out of the bag and set them on the countertop before sliding open a drawer in the large island.

"Chopsticks, forks or spoons?" she asked.

Can I fork you, then spoon?

I cleared my throat. "Fork, please." I could use chopsticks, but not well enough to take the risk. "And a spoon for the soup."

I took a moment to get a look around her apartment. "Nice place."

I'd expected somewhere bigger, but the view from the balcony was as incredible as mine. All of the seating was positioned to take advantage of it. The four stools that sat down one side of the island faced it. So did a huge sectional that dominated the room. Beside that was a bright pink bean bag that seemed out of place compared to the neutral blues and grays of the space.

"Thanks." She opened the soup containers, added spoons and pushed one across the island to me. "Beer?"

"Depends. Am I gonna get in trouble with the boss?" I picked up my spoon and scooped up a wonton to shove in my mouth.

She opened the fridge and pulled out two beers. As if she had something to prove, she glanced at me before cracking open one, then the other, with her bare hand. She slid one to me before picking up her soup and beer and gesturing over to the sectional.

"No need to be formal."

I wasn't much of a formal guy myself, so I sat down where she indicated, careful not to spill hot soup on myself.

The moment I sat down, something in the ceiling clicked. Through speakers all around the room came a male voice.

"*I parted her quivering legs with my hands, exposing her slick pussy. 'You're so wet for me, baby,' I said, keeping my voice low, just the way she liked it. I lowered my mouth to her wet heat and started to explore her with my tongue.*"

Andi had stopped dead still, her face bright pink. She hurried to lower her bowl and beer onto the coffee table in front of the couch and put her hand on my thigh.

"What are you—"

"I'm sorry, you're... I need to..." She looked down toward the couch.

I leaned over away from her and looked where she was looking.

"Oh."

She wasn't trying to touch my thigh, she had her

hand down between the cushions of the couch. She pulled out a small remote control and pressed a button, turning off the voice.

She cleared her throat awkwardly. "I like to listen to...audiobooks." Her face was adorably pink with embarrassment.

I cleared my own throat. "Yeah. Right. I like those too. I mean, not...the same as—" I pointed towards the ceiling.

"I figured," she said. "Not that there's anything wrong with men listening to romance. Or reading it."

"No, of course not," I agreed. "People can read whatever they want."

Shit, could this get any more awkward? "So, you were going to sort out a replay?"

She stared at me blankly for a moment before remembering why I was here. "Yes, hockey. Hockey replay."

Her response left me wondering what kind of replay she was thinking about. Maybe one of the audiobooks, with my tongue on her.

I shoved another wonton in my mouth before I said anything I might regret. While I chewed and swallowed, I rebooted my brain and reminded myself why I was here. "Where's your TV?"

Maybe it was in her bedroom. If I went in there, chances were I'd do something we'd both regret.

Or would we? She was a beautiful woman and I was undeniably attracted to her. The longer I sat here looking at the blush that still stained her cheeks, the more difficult it was to remember she was my boss.

Her expression unreadable, she pressed another button on the remote still in her hand. Slowly, a screen rose out of the coffee table in front of us.

"I keep it hidden, because I don't use it very often and it blocks the view," she explained.

Of course it did. That made more sense than my half-baked hope she'd invite me into her bedroom.

You're an idiot, Cam, I told myself. *As if a woman like her would be interested in you anyway.*

"That's a good idea," I said, my voice slightly too high for comfort.

I had a massive projector screen that slid up to hide in the ceiling that was perfect for movie nights. When it wasn't in use, it was tucked away and forgotten.

"It wasn't my idea," she said, but she didn't elaborate. Judging by the expression on her face, she preferred I didn't ask. That instantly made me curious, but I wouldn't pry.

She turned on the screen and started the replay of last weekend's game. She placed the remote down beside her and reached for her bowl and beer.

"Good choice," I said, nodding towards the screen. "This was a good game."

"Because you won?" she asked.

I grinned. "Any time we win is always a good time."

She glanced over and smiled. "I guess it would be."

I liked seeing her smile. I wanted to see it again. Quickly, I reminded myself I shouldn't.

This is just business, I told myself. *I'm just here to answer her questions, that's all.*

But it already felt like two friends sharing a meal and watching a game. There wasn't anything wrong with being friends, was there?

The kind of friend who wants to know how her pussy tastes, the back of my mind hinted unhelpfully.

I ignored it.

We sat back and watched the first period while we finished the first course and the first round of beers.

I hopped up when the horn sounded, taking our bowls to the kitchen and returning with rice, honey soy chicken, spring rolls and another beer each.

"You don't need to wait on me," she said, taking a plate and beer from my hands.

I shrugged and went back for mine. "My mom raised me to be polite and self-sufficient." I sat back down. "She's the kind of woman who won't let a kid, son or daughter, leave home without knowing how to cook and do laundry."

"You can do laundry?" Andi looked playfully skeptical.

"Sometimes I even remember to separate the whites from everything else," I said. "I can even fold socks so they don't get lost from each other."

"Impressive," she remarked. Her eyes shone like she was lightly teasing. Of course she was, anyone could fold socks.

On the other hand, tell my teammates that. Some of them wouldn't know how to pick up dirty socks, much less fold clean ones.

"Almost as good as these spring rolls," I said. "Try one."

She eyed me, picked one up and slid one end of it into her mouth. She closed her lips over it and bit down gently.

Her moan of appreciation made my balls tighten.

I swallowed heavily and forced myself to think

unsexy thoughts, and not picture those gorgeous lips around my cock, enjoying my taste.

"This is so good," she groaned.

"Yeah, it is," I said. So was the food. "Like I said, best in the city." It was also a diet buster, but I'd work out harder tomorrow to make up for it.

"You might be right," she agreed. "And no celery in any of it." She shifted her position on the couch as though she was physically uncomfortable, her expression bitter. She dropped her gaze.

"Who likes celery?" I asked carefully.

I didn't think this conversation was about the stringy vegetable. Instead, I got the impression someone in her life tried to make her feel guilty for enjoying food. Or for having curves.

As far as I was concerned, food was there to be enjoyed, and her curves were perfect. Anger flared up inside me, aimed squarely at anyone who dared to make her feel bad about herself.

Didn't she realise she was fucking gorgeous? I had a feeling she had no idea. Whoever it was that judged her made her judge herself.

She looked back up, her expression tinged with a hint of sadness. "I don't know. I don't like the way it gets stuck in my teeth."

I wanted to take that sadness away from her, but I had no idea why or how.

I managed to tear my eyes away from her, and back to the screen. "This is right where Flynn scored our second goal."

We skated into our positions, the camera panning across the ice and stopping behind us. I was leaning forward, body tense, eyes ready for the puck to drop.

I glanced over to see Andi, eyes on the screen, head tilted to the side. I looked back at myself, then back at her.

"Are you checking out my ass?" I grinned.

Her face went pink again. "No," she said quickly. "I'm checking out your stick." Her eyes widened. "Your *hockey* stick. I was looking at the way you were holding it. It's so long it looks..." She shook her head. "I'm just digging myself a bigger hole here, aren't I?"

I grinned bigger. "Not at all. My stick is big and needs to be handled just the right way."

Her tongue swept over her plump lower lip as her gaze dropped to my groin.

It seemed I wasn't the only one getting that vibe. If I was a gentleman, I'd excuse myself and leave before we got in too deep. But no one could ever accuse Cameron North of being a gentleman, so I hopped up and got us two more beers.

I sat back beside her and watched her watch me skate across the ice, slapping the puck to Flynn who flicked it past the goalie and into the basket.

"I feel like I should cheer," she remarked.

I raised my beer to her. "Cheers."

She clinked her bottle against mine and laughed. "You know that wasn't what I meant, right?"

I grinned. "I know, but I figured you weren't going to stand up and clap at the TV."

She raised her eyebrows, then placed her beer down in front of her. With a flourish, she stood, briefly applauded in the direction of the screen, then sat back down.

"I think that's the first time I've seen anyone golf clap to a hockey game," I remarked. "Usually people cheer and throw teddy bears."

"I'm sure they throw their panties at you too," she said.

"Jealous?" I teased.

She snorted like a cute little pig. Her eyes widened and she clapped a hand over her mouth. "I'm not jealous," she said from behind her fingers. "Why would I be jealous? People can throw whatever they like at you. Within reason. We wouldn't want our star winger getting injured by somebody's falling G-string."

The only thought I had in my mind at those words was her shimmying out of a dark red G-string and flinging it at me. Right before she lay back on my bed and spread her luscious thighs. I should definitely not have another beer, it was starting to go to my head, and my groin.

"For the record, no one throws their panties at me," I said evenly. "They throw them all at Nate. I think he collects them." He probably had a drawer overflowing with them. Puck only knew what he did with them. Frankly, I didn't want to know.

I didn't admit that some were aimed at me. Not literally panties, but longing looks and flirtation. I ignored all of it. That was a tangle I didn't want to get dragged back into. Not after the last time.

"What do you collect?" she asked.

That was a good question, what did I collect? Nothing much, apart from a bitter ex or two. Maybe chips on my shoulders.

"I never really found anything I wanted to collect," I said finally. My gaze lingered on her before I managed to turn my attention back to the game.

"Now this bit was controversial—"

Chapter Eleven

Andi

"How nice of you to join us." Quentin Welling looked down his long nose at me.

I slipped into the seat between him and my mother. "Nice to see you too, Dad," I said. I didn't bother to point out I was five minutes early.

Cynthia Welling clicked her tongue. "Don't be passive-aggressive, Andrea."

"Sorry, Mom," I said in my best placating tone. Would she prefer I was aggressive-aggressive? I could do a lot of damage with a salad fork if I wanted to.

She sniffed and picked up her menu. "I hear the seafood salad here is divine. And the Waldorf salad as well." She eyed me meaningfully.

I picked up my own menu and skimmed it. None of the items had prices. Exactly the kind of place my mother adored. She didn't want to think about spending money. According to her, if you had to think about it, you didn't have enough of it. Easy for her to say, when she was married to a self-made billionaire.

I hated the pretentiousness of places like this. Everyone was self-important and had some kind of agenda. Most of the people only ate here to be seen. Sure, the food was some of the best on the east coast, but Chantelle's was mostly about being rich and showing off.

"I think I'll have the ravioli," I said. "The one with beef inside. And some garlic bread."

"Andrea," Cynthia started. "Are you sure about that?"

I looked her straight in the eye and smiled. "I'm certain." I leaned over and placed my hand on hers. "But by all means, enjoy a salad."

I sat back and placed my hands in my lap. She rarely made direct comments about my weight, but I was done taking her indirect ones. I tolerated it from the people around me for too long, including Xander.

Quentin snorted. He never openly agreed with the things she said, but he didn't tell her to stop it either. No, he had his own ways of judging me.

"Something to say, honey?" Cynthia asked, her tone bordering on venomous.

"Nothing at all," he said, without looking up from his menu. "How's the hockey team going, Andi?" Unlike my mother, he rarely called me Andrea. Mostly because I didn't answer to it from anyone but her. And only from her because I knew she wouldn't budge. It wasn't worth starting a war over.

"Good," I said lightly. "How's the development side going without me?"

He finally lowered his menu and looked at me with eyes that matched mine. "Slowly," he said with a grunt of displeasure.

"Your father has already fired two people he hired to replace you," Cynthia said. "I keep telling him to sell that team and bring you back to the office where you belong. You have better things to do than play around with that nonsense. I have no idea what he was thinking." She rolled her eyes toward the ceiling.

"I'm enjoying the challenge," I said, trying not to bristle too visibly.

It didn't surprise me my father went through a couple of replacements already, but they probably quit, rather than being fired. He'd never been an easy man to work with, or for.

"But if the development side is suffering." Cynthia looked at Quentin meaningfully.

I felt as though I'd stepped between two land mines. Either way I moved, I risked being blown up.

Now that I thought about it, I couldn't remember a time when I wasn't placed in the middle of them, usually deliberately. One or the other expected me to take sides. Or at least mediate. That was what I usually did; try to calm them down until they found some kind of common ground.

But as I sat there with them, in the extravagant opulence of one of the most exclusive restaurants in Lowball Bay, I knew I didn't want to do it anymore. In the short amount of time since I'd started working with the Sea Dragons, I had more independence than I ever had before in my thirty years of life. Being away from them was good for me.

I caught the eye of a server. He nodded and hurried over to take our orders.

The ceasefire that lasted while he stood there ended when he moved away.

"I'm sure Andrea would like to return to work with you in your office," Cynthia insisted.

"Andi is where she is for a reason," Quentin

replied tightly. He seemed to be rapidly losing patience with the subject.

"What is that reason?" my mother snapped. "Because if we're losing money because of her absence, then this nonsense needs to end."

"The losses aren't significant," Quentin argued.

"Then why is she there?" Cynthia demanded. "Why in the everloving hell did you buy an ice hockey team?"

Could a hole please open up under my chair and swallow me? I thought.

The universe didn't oblige.

"Because she needed a challenge," Quentin replied. "The opportunity to further develop her skills. To succeed in business these days, a CEO has to be well-rounded."

"She'll be well-rounded all right," Cynthia muttered.

I stared at her. Had I heard her right? Had she really said something so bluntly mean about me?

She stared back at me. Blinked a couple of times. "That wasn't what I meant."

"I think it was," I said coolly. "I think you've been wanting to say that for a very long time. You know what? I don't give a shit."

"Andrea, language—"

I interrupted her. "My name is Andi, and I'll speak how I want to. I'm comfortable with the way I look and I don't give a fuck if you're not. That's your problem, not mine. I'm not going to sit here and take bullshit from you anymore." I shoved my chair back, letting the feet scrape painfully across the floor before I rose to my feet.

"Andrea," Cynthia hissed. "Don't make a scene."

"Let her go," Quentin said wearily. "You were out of line. You should know better than to comment on her appearance."

Cynthia turned back to him and the battle continued as I wound my way through the tables and out of the restaurant.

I will not cry. I will not cry.

I told myself that, over and over again as I walked across the road to the beach. Through a haze of tears, I managed to avoid being run over. That would have been a bad end to a frustrating afternoon.

I found an empty bench and sat, careful to avoid the pile of seagull droppings that decorated one side. My hands in my lap, I closed my eyes, breathed in the fresh sea air and attempted to breathe out my anger.

Manifest peace, I told myself. *Don't let her undermine you.*

I should be used to her shit by now, shouldn't I? I'd had a lifetime of her making not-so-subtle hints about everything she didn't like about me. Every disappointment and disapproval. Every toe I dared to put out of line.

Shouldn't I have thick skin by now? Why was this getting to me the way it was?

I buried my face in my hands and struggled to regain my composure. I knew the answer.

It started with Xander leaving, and extended to the first interaction with Cam. The way he looked at me like he wanted to eat me up, at the same time as he wanted to spit me out. He hated what he thought I was, even while the attraction sparked between us.

My insecurity made me wonder if it wasn't puck bunnies he didn't fuck, it was women like me. Women with curves. He wasn't the first man to think the way my mother did. He wouldn't be the last, either.

I wanted to tell myself he didn't. I saw the way he looked at me. The way his rare smiles were directed at me. The way he'd teased, laughed *with* me at my awkwardness when I talked about his stick.

I didn't think for a minute he bought it when I claimed I wasn't checking out his ass. I was absolutely checking out his ass. How could I not? It was so perfect and round in his hockey shorts. Even better in his jeans.

How many times did I have to remind myself we couldn't be more than colleagues? Nothing more than friends. I *shouldn't* have been checking him out.

I spent years struggling to maintain professional relationships with the people around me. Even when they treated me like I was only there because of who my father was. Some of them didn't like that about me, and some saw it as a foot in the door if they had a relationship with me.

Only people like Rafe saw me for who I was. Smart, competent and professional.

Maybe my mother was right and I should step away from the team, before I screwed everything up.

On the other hand, I could prove everyone wrong instead. I lowered my hands from my face and curled them into determined fists.

Yes, that was exactly what I'd do. I'd prove to everyone I had what it took to be the best damn team owner the Sea Dragons ever had.

Chapter Twelve

Cam

I couldn't stop thinking about Andi Welling. Everything I did these days, she was in the back of my mind. Or the front.

Now I was starting to see her everywhere I went. I blinked and looked again.

It took a moment to realize the adorable redhead on the bench was actually her.

The breeze blew her hair back off her face. Her blue eyes faced the ocean, glazed like she saw nothing.

In the late fall sunlight, the freckles on her skin stood out more than usual. Today's sweater was forest green, worn over black trousers and black ballet flats.

All of that I noticed immediately, but what made

me stop and stare was the expression on her face. I'd seen her nervous, annoyed and amused, but never apprehensive. She looked as though someone stripped off a couple of layers of her confidence and left her sitting alone on a bench by the beach.

"Hey." I sat down beside her, giving her a few inches of space if she didn't want company. I winced, realizing I sat in seagull droppings, but didn't move to stand again.

She glanced over at me as if she wasn't surprised to see me. "Hey. Are you stalking me?"

"No. I like to come down here and clear my head. But if I was going to stalk anyone, it would be a cute redhead."

She tilted her head at me, her expression one of cautious curiosity. "Is that your type?"

Was it? If you'd asked me a few weeks ago, I would have said I didn't have a type. I took each day and each person as they came. Since I met her, I kept picturing her hair fanned out on my pillow, blue eyes intent on me.

It might be the craziest thing in the world and it might be wrong, but Andi Welling was my type.

"It might be," I said. "What about you? Do you have a type? Let me guess. Wears an Armani suit and holidays in Bermuda every year."

Her nose wrinkled adorably. "I suppose that's expected of women like me. Find a nice man who works in an office, and have babies. Spend the rest of my life organizing charity galas and having tea parties with other women like me. For added excitement, maybe the occasional fling with a hot pool boy."

"You don't want any of that?" I asked. She seemed weary.

She sighed and looked back out at the waves. "I used to think I did. I used to think other people's expectations of me were accurate."

"And now?" Was this the source of her sadness the other night? "You've decided you want to give it all up and go to work on a fishing boat?"

She glanced back at me and laughed. "That's strangely specific, but no. I don't think I'd make a very good deckhand. I'd want to throw all the fish back."

"I can imagine you doing that. Scooping them all up one by one and throwing them overboard." I mimed throwing a fish.

"Until the rest of the crew throw me overboard." She mimed grabbing someone and tossing them sideways.

"Only to be rescued by the next passing boat," I said. "Maybe a luxury yacht."

Her smile faded. "Maybe I'd prefer a small rowboat with chipped paint to a luxury yacht." Her gaze lingered on me.

"If your type isn't an executive who wears a suit every day, you might prefer a regular guy." Was I trying to suggest I was her type? Was I a chipped paint kind of guy? I was rough around the edges at the best of times. On the outside and the inside.

"Come with me," I said. I got to my feet and held out my hand to her.

She hesitated, but took it and let me help her stand before letting it go again. For that brief moment, her skin was warm on mine, fingers small and elegant. A contrast to my big hands and rough, calloused skin.

I wanted to lace my fingers in hers and lead her to the sidewalk that ran along the edge of the beach. Instead, I kept my hands by my sides and walked with her.

Something about this, walking side by side, felt natural. Normal. Like we'd done this a million times before. No one we passed looked twice at us. No one stopped to remind us she was my boss and we shouldn't be walking like this on a Thursday afternoon.

If they had, I wouldn't give a shit anyway.

"What are we doing?" she asked when we stopped on the edge of the Lowball Bay Pier.

"That's up to you," I said. "We can get some cotton candy and see if I can win you a giant teddy bear. Or we could go on the Ferris wheel. Or," I gave her a challenging look, complete with a raised eyebrow, "we could go on the rollercoaster."

"Rollercoaster, without doubt," she said with no hesitation.

"You like a wild ride?" I knew she wouldn't miss the innuendo.

Her face turned pink, all the way up to her ears. She was so stinking adorable I could have kissed her then and there. My gaze tracked her tongue as it slid across her lower lip.

This woman.

"I've never been on the rollercoaster before," she said. "I've always stuck to the safe rides." Yeah, she was definitely not just talking about amusement rides.

"Then it's time to do something different," I said.

I led her over to the ticket booth and bought two tickets before she could insist on buying her own.

She was going to, I saw it on her face, but I was doing this for her.

Okay, for myself too. I'd lived in Lowball Bay for a handful of years and I never rode the rollercoaster either. What took me so long? I didn't know. Maybe I was waiting for the right moment. The fact it was now, with her, was a coincidence. Right? Yep, definitely.

"I'll buy the cotton candy after we ride," she said. "Unless you lose your lunch." It was her turn to give me a challenging look.

"Me?" I poked myself in the chest with my thumb. "Not gonna happen. You might lose yours."

"Mine is staying exactly where it is." She patted her belly.

We stepped over to the gate and I gave our tickets to the attendant. Tall and slender, he made eyes at Andi until I glared at him. She was riding me... *With* me.

He opened the gate and let us through.

I looked over the empty carriages before leading her to the green one. It was several shades brighter than anything I'd seen her wear, but it seemed to suit her.

She didn't say anything as she followed me in and settled down on the seat beside me.

I reached up to pull down the safety bar before the attendant locked it in place.

"Last chance if you want to get off," I said. Again with a deliberate choice of words.

"Scared?" she teased. Was it my imagination, or did her eyes darken at this innuendo?

"Of rollercoasters? No way." Of having her tear my heart out of my chest and throw it into the waves? Maybe. Of an amusement ride? No.

"Then why are your knuckles white?" She nodded down at the grip of my fingers on the safety bar.

I loosened them and rolled my back against the seat. "Couldn't be more comfortable. If I had a pillow, I'd fall asleep here."

She started to laugh, but the wind dragged it away as the carriage lurched forward and began its ascent up the first incline in the track.

Slowly, like it was dragging out the moment to increase the tension, the carriage chugged upward. The closer it got to the top, the faster my heart raced. The adrenaline rushed like before every game. The anticipation of what was to come.

"Hold on tight," I said when we reached the top. With a surge of speed, we thundered down the other side.

She let out a squeal of laughter which continued until we reached the next incline and slowed again.

"I should have done this sooner," she said. "I need to take more chances."

She wasn't just referring to this. Whatever led to her sitting on that bench, staring out at the ocean was part of something much bigger. Something I wanted her to be comfortable enough to confide in me. If not today, then someday.

What was I thinking? Someday? I hardly knew her, and we got off to a rocky start, but the more I saw, the more I wanted to see. Her mind. Her body. Everything.

I wanted to know all of her, the good and bad. And I wanted to share the parts of myself with her that I didn't share with anyone else.

I wasn't scared of rollercoasters, but I was scared of letting people in. I wanted to explain all of that to her. To let her know that my initial reaction to her was a reflex I'd developed to protect myself from being hurt. A reflex I wanted to put behind me.

"Everyone needs to take more chances." I glanced over at her.

Her cheeks were flushed with excitement, lips parted. Her hair whipped all around her face, but for once she didn't push it away. She was enjoying herself too much to care.

She was so incredibly gorgeous I forgot where I was for a few moments. Right until the carriage reached the top and plunged down another steep descent.

A shout of surprise and excitement roared out of me, chased by another laugh from her.

I could have listened to her laugh all day. I'd never heard an uninhibited sound that made my balls want to jump right out of my lap. I wanted to make her laugh, to know she was happy, and living in and loving the moment.

This was why I never rode the rollercoaster before. It wouldn't have been the same if I shared it with anyone else. Not with my friends. Not with another woman.

No, this moment was for us. For Andi and me. As long as I lived, I'd remember this. The moment we both decided to take a chance and do something daring. Something neither of us had done before. Side by side, we'd taken a leap, and we were having the time of our lives.

It might only happen once, but it might also be the beginning of many. For now, I was content to enjoy the right here, right now. With her.

The carriage reached a third incline and chugged its way up to the top. It puttered along a flat section of track that reached out over the ocean. We couldn't have been more than twenty feet up in the air, but I felt like I was in the sky. Soaring through the clouds with a stunning redhead pressed up next to me.

The carriage wound around the track, towards the deepest dip on the whole ride.

I held my breath in anticipation.

I went on holding it when the carriage stopped right on the edge of the decline. The nose couldn't have been more than an inch or two from the downward drop. The wind whipped up around us. Silence fell, broken by the sound of voices from far below, and the crash of the waves against the posts of the pier.

When I expected a sudden plunge down, nothing came.

The car stopped at the very top of the rollercoaster.

Chapter Thirteen

Andi

"WELL...SHIT." I LOOKED STRAIGHT DOWN INTO the deep blue water.

We were a long way up. I hoped like hell they didn't expect us to climb out and jump. I wasn't sure if I could. I was trying to grab life by the horns and enjoy it, but this was too big a leap, literally and figuratively.

"At least we're not hanging upside down," Cam remarked. He peered past me, into the water.

"That makes me feel a little bit better," I admitted.

"Only a little bit?" He gave me a slight smile, broad enough to pop a dimple in his cheek.

I told myself my racing heart was due to being

stuck here, on a bright green carriage at the top of a rollercoaster neither of us had ridden.

I quickly realized why I'd never been on the ride before now. I was held back by my perfectly rational fear of being stuck at the top of a rollercoaster. It was the universe telling me not to take risks. I should have opted for the cotton candy and a giant teddy bear.

A few minutes on the ground with a friend should have been enough. I was furious with my mother and that led me to do something irrational. Something I was now starting to regret.

"I mean, we're still stuck here," I said. "I've seen videos of people who were stuck for hours. What if that happens now? We could be up here all night." My voice rose higher with every word.

"The view is stunning." He gestured around us, but his gaze was on me. "The sun is setting. We'll have a bird's eye view of a beautiful sunset."

"I'm more worried we'll have a bird's eye view of a beautiful *sunrise*," I said.

The plastic seat wouldn't be comfortable all night. Sooner or later, we'd get hungry and thirsty. And need to pee.

"We won't be up here that long. Right now,

they're working on a way to get us down." He sounded sure of that.

I leaned against him and tried to ignore the way the carriage rocked in the breeze. "Can I tell you something?"

"Of course." He put his arm around me and cupped my shoulder with his big hand. "Anything. Right now, you have my undivided attention."

I snorted softly. "It's not like you can get up and walk away."

"That's true," he said. "You might as well spill."

"This might come as a surprise to you," I said dryly, "but I don't really like not being in control. Sitting here and waiting for help, it's..." I shook my head.

"Difficult?" he offered. "Slightly helpless? I feel all of that too. But you know what, I'm just going to enjoy this. How often do you get to sit out here over the ocean? The air smells clean up here. There's no hustle and bustle of people. No coach to yell at me. No one wanting to take a selfie with me."

"So if I ask for a selfie, the answer is no?" I couldn't help asking.

"If you want to take a selfie, the answer is yes," he said. "But you're not—"

"A puck bunny," I finished for him. "What if I was?"

"I wouldn't be up here with you if you were," he said. His voice was suddenly tighter. Guarded.

"What happened?" I asked softly. I guessed he got burned, but I didn't know why or by whom.

"You still haven't googled me?" he asked.

"No, should I have?" I asked.

He pulled his phone out of his back pocket, turned on the screen and entered his name into a search engine. Without a word, he handed me the phone.

I glanced at him, but then down at the screen. There in front of me was a photo of him, I guessed from a couple of years ago. He was smiling into the camera, but his smile looked forced, like he really didn't want his picture taken.

In direct contrast, was a woman with short blonde hair, green eyes and a huge smile. She was leaning against him, her posture possessive.

The caption said her name was Clio George, actor and model. That figured, she was absolutely stunning. Her skin was flawless. My mother would have envied her figure. Hell, so did I. In theory, they were the perfect couple, attractive and famous.

"Scroll down," Cam said.

I glanced over at him, but did as he suggested.

My heart lurched. I had to swallow down a knot of unexpected emotion that felt a little like jealousy.

Clio was clearly pregnant, her hand on her belly. Like the first photo, Cam stood beside her like he wanted to be anywhere else.

"We hooked up after that first photo," he said. "It seemed like the thing to do at the time. Star hockey player, gorgeous model, we were supposed to be the perfect fit, or some bullshit."

"And then she got pregnant," I whispered.

"And then she got pregnant," he agreed. "The longer we were together, the more I came to realize she was only with me because of who I was and what I could do for her career. Or what she thought I could do." He shrugged.

"So you have a kid?" What was he doing here with me then? He should be buying cotton candy for his child, and winning giant teddy bears for them. Were they old enough to learn to skate? Would he teach them?

I had a feeling any child of his would learn to skate right after they learned to walk. And hold a stick right after that.

He grunted in response. "Nope. Turns out it wasn't mine. The other guy insisted on a paternity test to prove it wasn't his and it turned out it was. Joke was on him, I guess."

He pressed his lips together so tight, his skin turned white. His brown eyes were unfocused, thinking back, obviously to a place he didn't want to think about any more. A place when a woman had pushed the knife into his heart and twisted the blade.

Why did I picture her laughing while she was doing it? Maybe it was as hard on her as it was on him.

"Shit," I whispered. "That must have been..." I had no words. What he must have gone through. Thinking the baby was his, only to have that taken away. It was far worse than having someone pack up and leave without a word. What Xander did didn't even come close to this. He must have felt utterly betrayed.

"It was a relief," he admitted. "I wanted to be a good dad, but not with her. Not for someone who couldn't see past my job and how much money I had in the bank. Not for someone who would have spent the rest of her career selling herself as wife of Mr. Cameron North. Mrs. Clio North, puck bunny."

He didn't bother to hide his bitterness.

I couldn't blame him. What sort of person does that to another? Maybe she really thought the baby was his, but if there was any doubt, she should have been honest with him. I couldn't imagine lying like that to anyone, especially not when a child was involved.

"That explains why you're so—" I said, trying to find the right words.

"Grumpy?" he suggested. "Cranky? Angry?"

"Careful," I said finally. "You got screwed over. If you weren't guarded, I'd be surprised and confused." I let the silence fall again for a few moments.

"The night we met, you thought I was like that," I said. "That I was just there to have my moment in the sun."

"Something like that," he agreed. "Beautiful women make me extra nervous."

I snorted softly. "You must have known I'm not a model. I mean, look at me." I waved a hand at myself.

"I am looking at you," he said, his voice pitched low. "Why wouldn't you be a model? You're absolutely fucking gorgeous." He tangled his fingers in my hair. He gripped it a little tighter before he leaned over to brush his lips over mine.

The rollercoaster car wasn't the only thing that stopped right then, my heart did too. I couldn't believe Cam was kissing me, of all people. Nor could I believe the jolt of electricity that snapped between us, all the way through my body and down into my core.

I missed the touch of his lips the moment he pulled back.

"I'm sorry," he muttered before slipping his arm from around me. He didn't make any attempt to move further away, so our arms still touched, but his walls were back up. His expression was as guarded as the first time we met. Not as hostile, but just as careful.

"Don't be," I said quickly. "We both got caught up in the heat of the moment."

Was that all it was? We were feeling close and shared a kiss? An incredible, electrical kiss that I wanted to do over and over again. But just one kiss.

"Yeah, I got carried away," he said. "I don't talk about Clio to many people. The guys know, Nate, Blake and Flynn, and Coach Lambton. Zack, unfortunately." He grimaced. "Otherwise, it's a piece of my past I'd rather stay in my past. I probably shouldn't have told you about it."

I handed back his phone. "I'm glad you did. Sometimes it's good to talk about things. You know, get them off your chest." His chest was muscular, but even muscular chests struggled with the weight of things like that.

"What else are friends for, if not to share things so they don't live rent free in your brain?" I asked.

"Friends, right," he said. He scratched above his eyebrow with his thumb. "You would have found out sooner or later. When you got curious and decided to look me up."

"You're certain I would have done that," I said lightly. The moment had gotten a little heavy and needed a sprinkle of levity to bring it back before it got too much.

"You definitely would," he agreed, teasing lightly now. "You strike me as the curious type. The kind who needs to know everything about everything and everyone around her."

"Did you just call me a control freak?" I asked, pretending to be offended.

"I think you admitted to being one," he pointed out. "Something about not wanting to be helpless."

"There's a difference between being stuck at the top of a rollercoaster and being nosy about people," I said.

"There's a difference between being nosy about people and wanting to learn about the people who work for you," he replied.

"There might be," I said. "But I prefer to get to know people face-to-face. Anyone else who looked at those photos might have come to a different conclusion than what the actual truth is."

They might have thought Cam and Clio had a happily ever after with their beautiful child. From the sound of it, that might have been the case. Not the happy ending, but if the child was his, it would definitely have been beautiful.

"I guess so," he said, his voice soft again. "Like anyone who found out your father gave you a hockey team might perceive you as a spoiled little rich girl."

"Is that how you see me?" I narrowed my eyes at him.

"I—"

Before he could respond to that, the carriage lurched a few inches back, before grinding forward and sliding down the incline.

All I could do was hang on, and wait for the ride to end.

Chapter Fourteen

Cam

Nate grinned. "You kissed the boss?" The last word came out as a choked laugh. "Bro—"

I dropped my chin and shook my head. "I know. It was a dumbass thing to do."

In the moment, it seemed right. One minute, we were having an honest conversation and the next my lips were on hers. She tasted like pure heaven. Soft and sweet, with a hint of herbs.

The only taste in my mouth now was regret. Okay, she hadn't pulled away, or gotten angry, but why would a woman like her want to be kissed by a guy like me? She could have any man she wanted. She was brilliant, beautiful and sexy as hell.

And me, I was a bitter, grumpy asshole on the verge of retirement from the only thing that had any real meaning in my life. I didn't want to think about what came after. Endorsement offers were still coming in, but that wasn't something I expected, or even wanted, to keep doing forever.

How many times could a guy have a photoshoot in his underwear anyway?

"It just happened," I said finally.

"If there's anything we know about you, it's that things don't just happen," Flynn reasoned. "You wouldn't have kissed her if you weren't thinking about it."

I tilted my head and looked at him through one eye. "I can be spontaneous."

He looked back at me for a moment before leaning over to tie up the laces on his skates.

"I can," I argued. I looked at Nate and Blake to back me up.

Nate was too busy trying to hold back a laugh, and Blake was grinning like an idiot.

"Fine," I said darkly. "I'm not always sponta-neous. But this was spontaneous. One minute we were having a conversation about Clio—"

The laughter faded.

"You told her about Clio?" Blake asked. "What did she say?" His brow was corrugated in sympathy, his tone careful, not wanting to overstep the line.

In the past, I made it clear I didn't want to talk about Clio, but I'd invited the topic into the locker room, and I couldn't back away from it now. Fortunately, it didn't evoke the same pain as it used to.

"What do you think she said?" I rubbed a hand over the back of my head.

"She thought you were a dumbass for falling for that bitch?" Zack offered from the other side of the locker room.

He was right, but I flipped him off. I was a dumbass where she was concerned. I wasn't going to admit that to him.

I lowered my voice and said, "Andi felt bad for me."

"And then you kissed her?" Nate asked.

"I got caught up in the moment." I pushed my foot into one of my skates. "We were stuck at the top of a rollercoaster, having a deep and meaningful conversation. I acted without thinking. It won't happen again."

"Sounds romantic," Blake said. "Did you ask them to stop the rollercoaster right there?"

I stared at him. "Of course not."

"Do you think she asked for the rollercoaster to be stopped?" Flynn rested his hands on his thighs.

He looked like a father wanting the honest truth from his errant child.

"No," I said, immediate and firm. "She had no idea we were going on the rollercoaster until we did. Neither did I. It was—"

"Spontaneous," all three of them said at the same time.

"Exactly," I said. "I saw her sitting there by herself, clearly needing a friend. I decided to be that friend, if she'd let me."

"Seems to me like she wasn't the only one who needed a friend," Flynn said.

"Sounds like more than friendship to me," Nate said. "If you ask me, I'd say Cam has a crush."

"Lucky no one asked you," I retorted.

"Of course they did." He grinned. "They didn't say the words, but the intention was there. Right, Blake?"

"I didn't ask, but I came to the same conclusion," Blake said. "Cam definitely has a thing for the boss. Personally, I think they'd be cute together."

"I agree." Nate nodded. "I vote that Cam should go for it." He raised his hand.

"I vote that too." Blake raised his own hand. "What do you think, Flynn?"

"I think you should stop talking about me like I'm

not here," I said. "It might surprise you to learn that none of you have a vote in my love life."

Nate and Blake shared looks of mock shock, mouth open, eyes wide.

"Can you believe that?" Nate asked. "We don't get a vote?"

Blake shook his head and raised his finger. "You're going to have to give me a minute to get my head around this." He screwed his eyes shut for a few moments, then nodded slowly. "Okay, I tried, but I can't. I vote that we get a vote in Cam's love life."

Zack walked past on his skates, heading out to the rink for training. He stopped beside us and gave us all a long look, like we were lab specimens gone wrong. Germs in a petri dish that should be thrown in a hot dishwasher as quickly as possible. And only handled while wearing thick, long gloves.

"You guys are idiots. Being on the same team with you is embarrassing." He curled his lip at us and looked disgusted.

"Feel free to leave then." Blake grinned and gave him a go away gesture with his fingers. He looked completely unmoved by anything Zack had to say. Like everything else in his life, he let it roll off him like the proverbial water off a duck's back.

If he took anything seriously, I never saw it.

Sometimes I wished I could have a not-give-a-shit attitude like him. I needed to stop letting things get to me.

Zack rolled his eyes, sneered and stomped past. He muttered something that sounded a lot like, "Fucking dickheads," before stepping out onto the ice.

Apparently I wasn't the only one who took things too seriously. If anyone needed to take the stick out of his ass, it was him. What was his problem anyway? So far, I hadn't managed to figure it out. It was possible he didn't like us, but that was unlikely. We were very likable. Right?

"About that vote," Blake started. He frowned like he was serious, but a smile tugged at the corners of his mouth, just visible under his beard.

"No," I said. "No voting on who gets a vote about my love life. Which, for the record, is non-existent. It was just a kiss and it's not going to happen again."

Only— I couldn't get the way she felt and tasted out of my mind. I wanted more, and I couldn't have it. The best thing, the only thing, I could do right now would be to put her out of my mind. And make sure I was never stuck on a rollercoaster with her again. Because if I was, I might kiss her again, and if I did I might not stop.

"But you want it to," Flynn said softly.

"It doesn't matter what I want," I said. "If she needs a friend again, I'll be that for her. That's it. She owns the team. You know what people would say if we got involved."

They'd spread it all over social media and make it into something that it wasn't. Like they had with Clio. Like they did any time any of the guys got involved with anyone. They circled like a school of piranha, ready to descend on us and rip us apart for their own amusement and profit.

The only regret I ever had in going pro was becoming the target of monetized gossip. If I had my way, it would be illegal.

"They'd say *'Lowball Bay Sea Dragons forward has steamy relationship with property development heiress,'*" Coach Lampton said. He walked towards us, his eyes on his phone. "That's what it says, right here." He tapped the screen, then turned his phone around to show me.

On the screen was a photo of Andi and me getting onto the rollercoaster. We were smiling together. The second photo showed us stopped at the top. A third showed us closer together, my fingers in her hair, lips on hers.

All of the photos were grainy, and the last one

could have been anyone, but put all three together like a series of events, it was clearly both of us.

Fuck.

"Fuck." I closed my eyes, hoping the image would be gone when I opened them again. It wasn't.

"According to this, you were making out and couldn't keep your hands off each other," Coach said. He looked up at me and raised his eyebrows.

"It was one kiss," I muttered. "It won't happen again."

Not after I was the asshat who offended her by suggesting people might see her as a spoiled little rich girl. The only one spoiling anything was me, spoiling the moment with my thoughtless words.

She made quick excuses once we had our feet on the ground and left. It was for the best. I couldn't screw up if she wasn't talking to me.

I hoped like hell she wouldn't insist on me being traded to another team, just to get rid of me. I didn't think she was petty like that, but there was a time when I didn't think Clio was either.

The back of my mind, my cock and my balls all conspired to agree that Andi was nothing like Clio. There might have also been a couple of thuds in my chest that joined that unhelpful chorus. Apparently only the front of my brain was on my side now.

"Tell that to the PR department." Coach shrugged. "That's their domain. Mine is getting your asses out there on the ice to train." He nodded to the other guys. "Get out there. North, the PR department wants to see you after training."

I groaned inwardly. This, right here, was a really good reason not to be spontaneous.

We could have ignored the photos of us spending time together if there wasn't a photograph of our kiss. People would move on from friends hanging out together at the pier. If they thought there was something more juicy going on, they'd be invested. They'd think they were entitled to know everything that went on behind closed doors. If that was nothing, they'd make something up.

It was nothing I couldn't handle if I had to, but my stupid ass hadn't thought about the impact on Andi. I hadn't thought about anything but wanting to taste her mouth. If I'd taken a moment to consider the consequences, I would have stopped myself. If that meant standing up, rocking the carriage and jumping off the side into the ocean, it would have prevented the coming shit storm. Right now that was at category one, but I had the sinking feeling it would pick up momentum.

"It might be time for another one of Blake's

naked runs around the outside of the arena," Nate deadpanned. "People would forget Cam like that." He snapped his fingers.

"I'm down for that." Blake grinned.

As far as I knew, he'd never run naked in public, but if anyone would do it, it would be him. None of us were shy about our bodies, not after sharing locker rooms for so long, but baring everything in public would give the PR department a migraine.

Not to mention, he'd be dumped by the team in about two seconds flat, and never play professional ice hockey again. Blake wouldn't give up his career for a few moments of public nudity.

I hoped.

"No one is running naked around the arena," Coach said. "Don't be distracted by this shit. Let the PR department deal with it and you guys deal with your jobs." To me he added, "I suggest you be more discreet next time."

He moved away before I could say there wouldn't be another next time. Judging by the look on his face, he was thinking the same thing the other guys were.

Of course there would be a next time, it was just a question of when.

Chapter Fifteen

Andi

Without glancing up, I pointed a finger at Rafe. "Don't say anything."

"Me? I wasn't going to say a word."

I looked up from my laptop where I'd been doom scrolling and cocked an eyebrow at him.

He stood with a hand pressed to his chest, over his heart, trying to look innocent.

Innocent, my ass.

"Yes, you were. I know you better than that. You can never resist."

He sank down into the chair on the opposite side of the smaller, more elegant desk I'd had installed in my office. "Fine, but only because you invited me to speak my mind."

"I don't think I invited you." I frowned slightly. "It was more... giving in to the inevitable."

He huffed slightly. "I can be quiet when I have to be."

My second eyebrow joined the first, arching in playful disbelief.

He raised his hands in surrender. "Fine, I'm happy to offer my opinion to anyone who'll listen. Which is usually you. In this case my opinion is—" He paused for dramatic effect. "Good for you. Why shouldn't you be kissing a smoking hot hockey player on the top of a rollercoaster at the pier? Or anyone else, for that matter. You deserve to be happy, especially after what Xander pulled. What sort of man moves out without saying anything? One without balls, that's who. He needs to grow a pair. You know who I bet already has a pair? Cam North. But I'm sure you know all about that. Did you get a feel?"

I shook my head at him. "No I didn't, but if I did I wouldn't tell you. Cam North's balls are none of your business."

Hell, they were none of mine either. He'd made that clear enough when he accused me of being a spoiled little rich girl. He was quick enough to walk away once he got down off the ride. He looked as though he couldn't wait to be anywhere but there. I'd seen that expression on Xander's face often enough, though I hadn't realized it until right then.

In retrospect, I wondered how the hell I missed such obvious warning signs. Yes, I was busy, but I was willfully oblivious as well. I didn't want to see what was right in front of me. If I did, I would have had to admit the relationship was over a long time ago.

"Fine," Rafe said. He caught the look on my face and sighed. "*Fine.* I'll have to find someone else to live vicariously through."

"You do that," I said. "Isn't your anniversary coming up soon?" If there was anything that could distract Rafe from my doomed love life, it was talking about his happy marriage, and spoiling his partner.

"Jacoby and I are thinking of having a big party," he said. "The whole team could come." He hesitated for a moment before saying, "We could have a big Christmas party with lots and lots of mistletoe."

That sounded appropriate for them. They were happy and they wanted everyone around them to be happy. On the night, they'd make it their mission to put as many couples together as they could. And Rafe would probably take credit for each and every one of them. Not in an arrogant way, because I didn't think he had an arrogant bone in his body, he just wanted to spread joy and bask in it.

"I'll remember not to stand under any," I said.

He pressed his lips together and gave me a look. "You need to stand under mistletoe more than anyone I know. You kissed Cam North, but you look like someone kicked your puppy." His eyes widened. "Was he that bad?" In a whisper he added, "Did he have bad breath? That's it, isn't it? I knew he couldn't be perfect. Did he eat onions right before your lip lock?"

"No, he did not eat onions," I said. "He doesn't have bad breath." He'd tasted like coffee with a hint of something savory, like meat and cheese. It was warm and pleasant, like a hug after a huge orgasm. Like spooning his hard body all night long.

Like... I didn't want to admit it to myself, but Cam North tasted like home.

"What is it then?" Rafe pushed. "Is that all those photos?"

"There's only three, and they're all over social media," I said. "Along with approximately one hundred and seventy-three different theories about our relationship. They start with suggestions he's sleeping with me so he doesn't get kicked off the team, and end with him being an alien."

"You know you've made it when the Internet accuses you of being an alien," Rafe said with a grin.

"I guess I haven't made it yet," I said wearily. "Most of them suggest I'm using him."

That stung worst of all. After the conversation with my parents, he made me feel good about myself for a while. Now, I felt like I was back at square one. Behind square one maybe, because accusations of using people who work for you, tended to stick.

Rafe grimaced. "The Internet is such a bitch. Those of us who know you, know you're not like that. The PR department is working to turn the story around. I heard a rumor they're bringing in someone special just for this."

"Because this is a particularly bad dumpster fire," I said with a sigh. "I never should have gone on that rollercoaster."

"I said the same thing about Jacoby when we first met," Rafe said. "We're both so different, it was wild for a while. But we stuck in there, and look how we turned out. I've almost managed to convince him *Star Trek* is the best franchise ever." In a loud whisper, he added, "He still swears it's *Star Wars*."

I shook my head at him. "That's quite the obstacle you had to overcome. Especially when the reality is, it's a tie between *Vampire Diaries* and *Stargate*."

Rafe raised a hand to his lips in mock horror. "Clearly I haven't educated you properly. It's time we had a *Star Trek* marathon."

We were interrupted by the sound of Cam, leaning against the door frame and clearing his throat.

Rafe swiveled around in his chair. "Perfect timing. Help me to settle this issue once and for all. *Star Trek* is better than *Vampire Diaries* or *Stargate*, right? I mean, they're all great, but *Star Trek* is by far the most superior franchise of all time."

"I'm more a *Supernatural* guy, to be honest," Cam said.

Rafe raised a hand in front of him and sniffed. "You're both dead to me." He shook his head and smiled. "But you're both invited to the *Star Trek* marathon. I'll convert you yet. In the meantime, coffee." He pushed himself to his feet and headed towards the door. He stopped in front of Cam and gave him a Vulcan salute.

Cam smiled, held up his hand and returned the gesture.

Rafe turned back at me and grinned. "He's a

keeper." He hurried out of the office before I could respond.

"He's such a geek," I said. "I guess that's why we get along, I'm a nerd." I gestured for Cam to come inside and take the seat Rafe just vacated. "I take it you've seen the photos."

Cam sat back in the chair and crossed his legs. The ankle of his track pants rode up, revealing brightly colored socks, covered in what looked like dancing penguins.

He rubbed his stubbled chin, brown eyes filled with regret. "I have. I've just come back from speaking to PR. Apparently they're hiring my sister to deal with this...situation."

I sighed and rubbed my temples with my fingertips. "I'm sorry. This whole shit storm is a mess already. It shouldn't have happened."

"I'm the one who's sorry," he said softly. "If I hadn't kissed you..."

"It takes two to share a kiss," I said. "You didn't hear me objecting, did you?"

"No, I didn't," he admitted. "But if I hadn't done it, they wouldn't be saying the things they're saying about us. About you. They wouldn't have to involve my sister." His lips twisted to the side in annoyance.

"Is that the real problem here?" I asked lightly.

"The fact they're bringing your sister in to deal with what we did?"

Was he more concerned that family was getting involved than he was about the hate the Internet was dumping on me? I couldn't even start to get my head around how I felt about that. Of course, family was important, why would you put a virtual stranger in front of them? Especially one who was a one-woman dumpster fire when it came to relationships.

"My sister is good at what she does," he said.

He closed his eyes and exhaled slowly out his nose. "After Clio and I ended it, social media had a bunch of shit to say about me. They claimed I abandoned her. There were only two ways to deal with it, tell the truth and drag our whole relationship through the mud, or wait and hope like hell it blew over. I chose the second option. I stayed away from social media and ignored it until it went away. Before that..." He shook his head, opened his eyes and looked directly into mine.

"I don't want you to have to weather that storm because of anything I did. The things they're saying about you are a whole lot worse than anything they're saying about me."

"I know," I said softly. "They always are." He was the hockey hero who got caught playing tonsil hockey with his boss. And I was the curvy woman taking advantage of him. Because of course, a man like him wouldn't voluntarily kiss a woman like me. Except that he had, and I wished he would again.

I leaned forward and rested my elbows on the desk. "I've been reading things about myself since before I started working for my father. If I let it get to me, I'd be curled up in the corner, crying. But I can't, and I won't. Because the people saying those things? They don't know me. They don't know you. They just have nothing better to do than make up bullshit. Unless you're an actual alien?"

He looked surprised for a moment, then grinned. Did he have to be so gorgeous?

I wanted to kiss him again. I wanted to lick the dimple in his cheek. I wanted to lick my way down his body to his cock. I wanted to wrap my mouth around him and taste him, while he writhed, moaned and gripped my hair.

"As far as I know, I'm not an alien," he said. "Are you?"

"Probably," I said with a laugh. "That would be ironic. They're saying everything but that."

"Give it time," he said with a knowing nod. "Unless you want the PR department to spread that rumor on purpose. I'm sure Alice would be only too happy to do that for you."

"Let's call that plan B," I said. "Anyway, I didn't ask if you needed to see me for anything." I chastized myself. I was supposed to be a professional here.

"I wanted to see how you were, and to apologize again," he said. "I didn't mean to imply that I think you're a spoiled little rich girl. I don't think that, not at all. What I said about you being beautiful, I meant that. And smart. And competent." After a beat he added, "For an alien."

I snorted softly. "Thanks. I think." I held out my hand. "Friends?" For a moment, I thought he was going to refuse, but he gripped my hand.

"Friends." For some reason, he didn't look happy about it.

If I was honest with myself, neither was I. Friends was good. Friends was *safe*. Being friends might convince me I wasn't falling for him.

Chapter Sixteen

Cam

"Bro, bro, bro." Alice clicked her tongue and shook her head at me as if she was the older sibling, not younger than me by four years.

I gave her the side eye, but didn't stop chopping vegetables for my quick stir fry. "It's not that bad."

"It's definitely that bad." She tapped on her phone screen with one hand while taking a sip of wine with the other. My sister was nothing if not skilled at multitasking. "Have you read what people are saying?"

"That's your job," I said. "I've been avoiding reading anything about myself for the last few years." I sliced a carrot with a bit more force than necessary.

"Right," she said in that unapologetic way siblings got away with. "Well this is a different situation. You can bury your head in the sand if you want."

"I think I will, thanks." I tossed the vegetables into the wok and started to turn them over with my spatula. Again, with more force than necessary.

"Cam, you can't avoid this forever," she scolded.

"You just said I could." I glanced at her quickly before returning my attention to the wok.

"I lied," she said. "You can't bury your head in the sand forever. People have opinions, and opinions can make or break someone's career."

"I'll tell you where they can shove their opinions," I muttered. "Andi isn't using me and I'm not using her. We're just friends." Most of my friends didn't make my cock want to jump out of my pants, but sooner or later, he'd accept that she was off-limits.

"What?" Alice's tone made me turn and glance at her. "Bro, that was yesterday's news. Today, everyone thinks you'd be adorable together. In fact, the Internet has already given you a couple name. Candi. Isn't that cute?"

"We're not a couple," I said before returning my attention to the vegetables. "Like I said, we're just friends." Candi? Where did people come up with these things? Okay, it was kinda cute, but it was one kiss and now they'd decided we were, what? Destined to be together?

Maybe you are, the back of my mind said.

I couldn't tell you what my balls said, it wasn't coherent. It might have involved a party whistle and a bunch of confetti.

"Why are you bringing this up?" I asked. "If they're not saying bad things about us, then what does it matter? You can go back to your own clients, trying to make them look good."

"The Sea Dragons offered me an ongoing contract," she said easily. "I'm going to be around a lot more. That makes you my client. Also, I think you should milk this. If you're not a couple, where's the harm in letting people think you are? It'll be good for your image, and hers."

"You want me to pretend we're involved?" I turned off the heat and leaned my hip against the countertop to stare at her.

Who said we'd be pretending? my cock wanted to know. *I've never faked it before, I don't need to fake it now.*

I was starting to think my body was supplying too much blood to that part of me. I needed more in the head on my shoulders and less in the one in my pants.

"She's still the boss," I pointed out. "And I'm not going to play games with her just to please a bunch of strangers. Been there, done that. Fucked if I'm doing it again."

I turned back to throw rice and vegetables into bowls. I all but slapped one down in front of Alice and tossed a fork roughly in her direction.

Somehow, she managed to catch it without losing her grip on her wine glass or her phone.

"I'm not asking you to pretend without her knowing what's going on," Alice said. "I know you don't do sneaky."

I stabbed my fork into a piece of carrot. "No, I don't. I'm not going to pretend, with or without her knowledge." That was the end of the story, as far as I was concerned.

"Would you really be pretending?" She eyed me over a chunk of broccoli.

"What are you talking about?" I was more snappy than I intended. She was stepping too close to dangerous territory.

"I'm talking about the fact my oldest brother wouldn't go around kissing anyone if he didn't care about them," she said. "You do, don't you? That's why you're all prickly and defensive."

"I'm not defensive," I argued. Defensively.

She snorted like a pig with a head cold and a mouth full of food. "You're so full of shit."

"It takes one to know one," I said. Why not pretend to be grade school-aged again? Wasn't that what siblings were for?

She laughed. "That doesn't even make any sense." She stabbed the air in front of her with her fork. "Which is typical Cam."

"It is not," I protested. "I make perfect sense. Some of the time. I mean, most of the time."

"You were right the first time," she said. "Prickly, defensive and now deflecting. You must really like this woman."

"Me, deflect? Oh look, a seagull." I pointed my fork towards the window.

"You're such a dork," she said. "I'm not falling for the old seagull out the window trick."

"It used to get your attention," I grumbled.

"When I was three." She sipped her wine and shook her head at me. "You need to up your game if you're going to divert my attention."

"Chris Hemsworth just flew past?" I suggested. Yes, I was also a comic book geek from way back. So was Alice. She'd seen every Marvel and DC movie a hundred times each, at least. She was more than a little obsessed with the Australian actor who played

Thor. If he went past, she'd be out the door like a shot.

"Closer, but it lacks plausibility," she said. "Since, as far as I know, even he can't fly."

"You never know," I said with a nod. "If anyone could, it'd be him."

"No wonder you're so good at playing hockey," Alice said slowly. "You're good at keeping the topic of conversation away from the goal. Andi Welling being the goal."

"I figured," I said half under my breath. "Has it occurred to you that I don't want to talk about her?"

"It has, but I ignored the thought." Alice smiled. "Because the Internet wants to talk about you and her, so I do as well. Admit it, you like her. Putting aside the fact she's technically your boss, you're both consenting adults. As far as I know, there are no laws against you being together. So what's the obstacle?" She cocked her head and frowned. "Don't tell me, she doesn't like you."

"I think she likes me," I said. She didn't push me away when I kissed her. She kissed me back. She'd even made a soft little moan that made my dick twitch.

"Then what's the problem?"

What was the problem?

"For one thing, she's out of my league," I admitted. "You've met her, she's fucking gorgeous. Smart and successful."

"You never heard this from me, but some people would describe you that way." Alice wrinkled her nose. "Not me though. To me, you're just my dorky big brother who used to use my dolls as pucks."

I grinned. "Yeah, I did. I was a shit back then."

"I know. I'm still in therapy for it," she teased.

At least, I thought she was teasing.

"Then there's the fact the Internet hated us a couple of days ago," I said. "They might hate us tomorrow." Softly I added, "They might hate her tomorrow."

"So you want to protect her from trolls?" Alice concluded. "That's really sweet. Who knew you had that in you?" She grinned before biting into a green bean, which was covered in grains of white rice and sauce.

I raised my middle finger from my fork and flipped her off. "I can be sweet. Just don't go telling anyone. If people think I'm a grumpy asshole, they tend to stay away from me."

"It would be very good for your image if people knew you were sweet," she said. When I glared at her, she raised her hand in front of her, palm out.

"Okay, okay. I'll do my best to make sure they don't know the extent of how sweet you are. But seriously, have you spoken to her about this?"

"Of course I have," I said. "We agreed to be friends. That's all we're going to be, all right?" I looked at her sideways, sternly, waiting until she nodded her agreement.

"Fine," she said reluctantly. "But now people have grabbed hold of this scenario, they may not want to let go. They're going to keep shipping you as a couple until they latch on to someone else."

"They can latch onto Nate," I said.

There must be hundreds of guys more interesting than me. Thousands. I played hockey, and I was good at it. Apart from that, why would anyone bother gossiping about me? I was just a regular guy who was lucky enough to be living his dream, doing his dream job. That didn't seem newsworthy to me. Not unless you're a hockey mad kid, like I was, who wanted to know his dreams could come true too. Then, I supposed I had something to offer.

"The Internet prefers couples who last longer than an hour," Alice said dryly. "Besides, they already adore him for who he is. The team's resident playboy. They'd be surprised if he was seen kissing the same woman twice."

"Why does that not surprise me?" I asked.

If I acted the way he did, I'd be universally loathed by the monetized gossip machine. Nate always came off smelling like roses. Maybe because he was nice to reporters when they wanted to interview the members of the team. Whereas I preferred to glare and respond with one-word answers. Anything to keep them from coming back for more.

"The public loves to think they know famous people personally," Alice said. "And they love nothing more than to ascribe personalities to their favorite players. The grump." She gestured at me. "The Playboy. The serious, fatherly type."

"The asshole," I said thinking about Zack.

"The jokester?" she added. "Who might be misunderstood."

I made a face. "Or not so misunderstood, in some cases." Obviously, she was talking about someone else. There was no way in hell my sister would be interested in Blake Eastwood. If he so much as looked at her the wrong way, I'd rearrange his face.

"Either way, the Internet will have an opinion until the end of time," she said. "Just be aware they aren't done with you yet. While you're both involved with the Sea Dragons, they'll persist with rumors and speculation. You'll be under the proverbial micro-scope for a while."

"It might be time to consider retirement," I grumbled.

Alice stared at me. "You have it bad, don't you? You must have, or you wouldn't even suggest retiring from hockey. You'd really do that to save her from scrutiny?"

"Don't read too much into it," I said. "I was throwing out a thought, that's all."

"Oh, I'm reading all right," she said. "My big brother is in looove." She drew out the last word until she ran out of breath and had to stop. She sucked in another and grinned.

Love? It was too early to talk about love, but Alice wasn't too far off the mark.

Retiring never seemed plausible before, but now it wasn't completely off the table. If it helped Andi, how could I not at least consider it?

Chapter Seventeen

Andi

"WE CAN SEE EVERYTHING FROM HERE." I gestured for my mother to sit in an armchair near the plexiglass window. The team box was comfortable enough to accommodate even her particular needs.

Okay, that depended how particular she was on any given night. Tonight, she was quiet, clicking her tongue and looking displeased in general.

In other words, it was going to be a long night.

"So I see," she said, looking unimpressed. She perched on the edge of the chair and looked down at the crowds and ice.

I suppressed a sigh and sat beside her. "Thank you for coming to the game with me tonight. I thought maybe we could...I don't know, have fun."

She cast me a sidelong look. "I was curious to see what you do here."

Of course she was. She couldn't just enjoy a night out with me. Let loose for a while. Was she capable of having fun?

When I was a kid, she used to read to me a lot, but I didn't remember her sitting down with me to play. My father would, when he wasn't busy, but those instances were rare.

Mostly, I spent my time with Pia, or whichever nanny we had at the time. We went through two or three before my parents hired Bethany. She stayed with us until neither of us needed a nanny anymore.

I lost count of the amount of times I'd wished Bethany was my mother instead of Cynthia. Even though Bethany was paid to care, she seemed more genuine in her affection than my mother ever was.

We still kept in touch, texting and chatting from time to time. She worked for another family now, on the other side of the country. I missed her, but I swore if I had children, I'd never need someone like her. I wanted to be there for them myself.

"What did you think I do here?" I asked.

For all I knew, she assumed I'd learned to skate, and now spent my days whizzing around on the ice. Or maybe driving the Zamboni.

I won't lie, I'd considered asking to learn how to drive the big machine. It looked like fun. I saw no reason not to try, but for now I'd leave it to the experts. That was currently a man named Hank. Not much older than me, he was so grumpy, he made Cam look like a ray of sunshine. For some reason, all of the guys seemed to adore him.

I'd yet to hold an actual conversation with the man. Whenever I saw him, I said hello, but he usually responded with a grunt and a nod. I made a mental note to try harder.

Cynthia sniffed. "I have no idea. Apart from having inappropriate relationships with men who play games for a living."

It was impossible not to bristle at that. "I'm not having an inappropriate relationship with anyone. And playing hockey for a living is much more difficult than you think. It's a lot of hard work. Much more difficult than attending charity galas and tea parties."

I should know better than to bite, but I couldn't contain myself. If she'd come here to insult me, then she shouldn't have come.

"Are you suggesting raising money for charity isn't important?" she asked coolly.

"Of course it is," I said. "Which is why the team

does a lot of charity work and makes hefty donations. Giving back is one of the most important things we can do." This might be the only time we were on the same page about anything.

She sniffed. "Yes it is." Grudgingly, she added, "I suppose if them hitting a piece of rubber around ice with a stick leads to them doing good work, then it might be *somewhat* worth it."

I didn't miss her emphasis on the word 'somewhat.' Was it too late to have security remove her from the box and banned from the arena? It would create more trouble than it was worth, or I might give it serious consideration.

The only conflict I wanted to see tonight was the Sea Dragons taking on the opposition team, the Tangleville Tornadoes.

The last time the two teams played each other, the Tornadoes won. There was no reason to think they couldn't be beaten tonight. That was what Coach Lambton told me anyway. Since he knew what he was talking about, I took his word for it. Someday, I'd be able to make predictions based on my own knowledge, not that of someone else. For now, I'd rely on his expertise.

"Look, here comes the team." I pointed through

the window, as if she couldn't see the Sea Dragons step out onto the ice to warm up.

My gaze quickly found Cam, number twelve. He was having a conversation with Blake Eastwood, number three. Whatever he was saying, Blake seemed to find it hilarious. He tipped his head back and laughed before skating away in his goalie padding that looked awkward to me. He made wearing it look effortless.

Cam shook his head and skated after him.

His movement on the ice was so smooth, like he was born for it. My eyes followed him everywhere he went. I was drawn to him like a magnet. A moth to flame, might be a better analogy. If I wasn't careful, I was going to get burnt.

"He's the one who's compromised your reputation," Cynthia stated. She must have noticed my gaze glued to him. Or maybe she'd looked him up. She never could resist the chance to stick her nose in my business.

She'd say she cared, that was why she did it, but I was thirty years old. I didn't need my mother fussing over me like that anymore. Caring, yes, but not interfering. If that was her intention here, she could think again. The situation between me and Cam was complicated enough.

Friends, but seeing him down there, my clit throbbed. Being in the same arena as him made my pulse ratchet up. Even with rows and rows of seats, and plexiglass between us.

"I think it's the other way round," I said without glancing at her.

I'd seen the shift in public sentiment, but it didn't do much to ease my discomfort. The winds changed and changed back too often. Tomorrow, they could hate me for being here to watch him...I mean, watch my team. Where else would I be when they were playing?

No doubt, I'd get hate if I was absent. When it came down to it, all I could do was keep on keeping on and try not to screw up too publicly.

"All the more reason to return to working with your father," Cynthia said. "If the situation isn't tenable for you, why are you still here?"

"It's perfectly tenable," I said without flinching. "Remember the time you wore the same outfit to two different tea parties, on the same day? The scandal was absolutely shocking. And yet, you still attended a charity ball that night."

"It's hardly the same thing as kissing some hockey player on an amusement ride," she said.

"It's definitely worse," I said sarcastically.

Honestly, who in the world had time to give a shit what someone else wore, much less care if they wore it twice? On the same day, no less. As if she was supposed to do— What? Go all the way home and get changed into some other ridiculously expensive outfit, just so people wouldn't take photos and gossip?

That was a humongous waste of time and money. I had to commend her for donating her outfits after she wore them, so they weren't completely wasted, but I didn't care if anyone saw me wear the same jeans I was wearing right now, tomorrow, or next week. If that was the worst they had to say about me, let them.

"I know you don't take those things seriously—" she started.

"No, I don't, and neither should you." I held up a hand to her. "But you know what, you do you. I know you do good work raising money, and if different outfits help, then I say go for it."

"Thank you for your permission," she said dryly.

I gave her a watery smile. "You're welcome. I'm getting something to eat. Would you like anything? I made sure there was salad for you."

"Perhaps later," she said absently.

I nodded and walked the handful of steps over to

the food table that ran along the wall to the side of the room. It was covered with dozens of plates of food. More than enough for the families and management who occupied the box with us. Wives, girlfriends, parents and children of the players and coaches. All chatting, laughing and waiting for the game to start.

I eyed the salads, but decided to go for a hotdog instead. With ketchup and mustard, just how I liked them. I placed my hotdog on a small plate and carried it over to my seat.

Predictably, Cynthia cast her gaze at my choice of food. "You're not going to eat that are you?"

"Of course I am," I replied. "What else would I do with it?"

"Do you know what those things are made out of?" She looked disgusted. "And white bread? Honestly, Andrea." Her lips were twisted to the side like she couldn't comprehend that anyone would perceive this as food, worthy of being put into their body. As if the fact they were delicious didn't matter.

For love of puck, it wasn't like I ate this stuff for every meal, and twice on Sundays.

"They're made of tastiness." I smiled and picked up my hotdog before tilting my head to wrap my lips around the Frank that stuck out of the end of the roll.

At the same moment, I caught sight of myself on the big screen at the back of the arena and froze. Eyes wide, mouth around the Frank like I was doing something inappropriate to it.

The arena erupted into laughter. As if somehow I was caught giving a blowjob to a hotdog.

Hell, I was just eating. If I was a man, they wouldn't have had the camera on me like this. Of course not, sexualizing women eating was much more entertaining to narrow-minded people.

My face pink, I bit down on the Frank and lowered the rest of the hotdog away from my face. I chewed a few times and tried to swallow, but the chunk of Frank stuck in my throat, cutting off my airway.

My face turned red as I struggled to breathe. I shook my head, trying to suppress the fast building wave of panic. I was going to die here, choking on a hotdog. Shit, I didn't want to go like this.

My vision began to haze.

Beside me, my mother finally realized what was going on. She shot up in her seat and shouted, "She's choking! She's choking on a piece of hotdog!"

I didn't know who came up behind me, but a firm hand pushed me forward and slapped me hard between the shoulder blades. Once, twice.

The offending piece of Frank popped out of my mouth, flew right into the plexiglass and bounced before falling onto the floor at my feet.

I sucked in a huge gasp of precious oxygen. And another for good measure. I coughed a couple of times and took a sip of water when someone offered me a cup.

"I'm okay, I'm okay," I said between coughs. "I'm fine."

Except I was still on the screen. The entire arena had seen a Frank fuck my mouth before almost choking me to death.

The entire arena, including Cam, who was standing in the middle of the ice, staring at the screen along with everyone else.

Shit.

Shit.

"Shit."

I handed back the empty water cup, stood and grabbed up the rest of my hotdog before fleeing from the box.

Chapter Eighteen

Cam

Coach took one look at my face as I stepped off the ice. "Go," he said with a sigh.

I wasn't going to have my head in the game until I was sure Andi was all right, and he knew it.

Seeing her face on the screen like that, knowing she couldn't breathe, while the whole damn arena watched... My heart had stopped. Ached.

She could have died.

She could have died.

I bolted into the locker room and threw myself down onto a seat. In approximately half a second, I tore off my skates, cup and padding and ran for the door in my shorts and socks.

I all but flew down the corridor toward the elevator that led up to the private boxes. I skidded to a stop on the slippery floor, sliding the last foot before slamming, shoulder first into the elevator door.

I swore under my breath. That hurt like a bitch. I jammed my thumb down on the up button, holding it there until the doors slid open. I tumbled into the elevator car and jabbed at the button to close the doors.

Because I was in a hurry, they took at least three days to close. Of course it fucking did.

I'd started to jump out of the elevator and take the stairs, when they finally slid shut.

They barely started to open on the next floor before I was sliding past them and running to the team box.

I tried the door, but it was locked. I hammered it with my fist.

After a few moments, it swung open, revealing one of the arena security staff.

"Mr. North," she said politely.

"Where is she?" I looked past her, trying to see Andi, but I saw no sign of the gorgeous redhead or her wild curls.

"Where is who, sir?" The security guard stepped back, letting me in, but clearly confused.

"Andi Welling," I said quickly. "The team owner. She was here."

"Oh. I don't know, sir," the guard said politely. "She slipped out a couple of minutes ago." She gave me a funny look, and glanced out towards the ice. The game started, but I couldn't bring myself to care at the moment.

"Did you see what direction she went?" I asked impatiently.

"I'm sorry, no I didn't," the guard said. "Only that she was in a hurry to leave."

"You let her leave?" I stared. Andi could have died and they'd just let her walk away?

"I'm here to keep people out, not in," she said, starting to look irritated. Apparently she didn't appreciate the suggestion she wasn't doing her job right.

I might feel bad about that later, but like the game, I couldn't worry about that.

I spotted a woman sitting near the window, looking slightly pale and rattled. With barely a glance, I pushed past the guard and a handful of other people in the box.

"You're Andi's mother," I stated.

"Yes." She looked at me like she had no idea who I was and didn't want to know. "Yes, I am."

"Do you know where she went?" Why had she not gone with Andi? If it was my daughter, I wouldn't have left her side.

"I'm not familiar with the facility," she said. "I'm sure Andrea will be back soon. When she's pulled herself together."

"When she's—" I stared at this woman. She seemed more concerned with Andi's composure than her health or well-being. "Everyone in the arena saw what happened."

Andi looked horrified. Embarrassed. My heart fucking ached for her.

"I'm aware of that," Andi's mother said. "It was unfortunate timing."

"It's much better to choke and almost die when there's not a camera on you," I said sarcastically. Was that all she gave a shit about? That the whole world might see what happened? That millions of people would watch the footage and be talking about it?

Worse, they might only show the handful of moments when Andi had her mouth around the Frank. Knowing the Internet, they'd turn that into a meme in about thirty seconds flat.

This whole thing was bullshit.

"If you think I don't care about my daughter—" Mrs. Welling started.

"If you cared, you'd be looking for her right now," I said.

I gave her a scathing look before turning on my socked feet and marching back out the door. If Andi was still in the building, there was one place I might find her.

I didn't bother with the elevator, I headed straight for the stairs, taking them two at a time before I reached the level that held the executive offices. I thanked past me for keeping my key card in my pocket, because I needed it to swipe into the corridor at the very back of the building.

"Andi?" I called out. "Are you in here?" I trotted down toward her office and swiped my card to open the door.

At first, I thought the office was empty, then I saw her sitting on the leather couch under the window, her face pale in the light that came from the parking lot. Her cheeks were damp, eyes shining. On her lap was a plate with a half eaten hotdog on it.

"Hey," I said softly. "You okay?"

She sniffed and dabbed at her eyes with a tissue. "Yes. No. I don't know. You saw what happened."

I eased myself down beside her. "Yeah, I did."

"So did everyone else," she added.

"They all got an impromptu crash course in what to do if someone's choking," I said lightly.

She snorted softly, then blew her nose. "I guess it wasn't all bad then."

I placed a hand on her thigh. "People eat hotdogs every day. There's nothing to be ashamed of."

"People don't end up on a big screen every day," she said with a sniff. "As though I was trying to blow the Frank. I'm never eating a sausage again."

My sausage might have let out a whimper of disappointment at hearing that.

"You shouldn't let one dumbass with a camera put you off eating sausages," I said. "If you like eating sausages, then I think you should eat all the sausages you want."

"Lowball Bay *is* known for its world-class sausages," she said with a hint of wistfulness.

"So I've heard," I said, barely managing to hold back a smile. "You wouldn't want to deprive yourself of that sausagey goodness, would you?"

"I suppose not," she agreed.

My sausage cheered. My meatballs might have joined in.

I stroked the back of my hand down her smooth, damp cheek. Wiped away tears and brushed back her hair. "I was worried about you. When I saw you up there and realized you couldn't breathe, I couldn't breathe either. I couldn't do anything but watch. I've never felt so fucking helpless in my life."

She leaned into my hand. "I don't think I have either."

"You're not referring to the choking, are you?" I asked gently.

"I am, but not only that," she replied. "When I was looking back at myself, with a mouthful of sausage, I realized I'd always be under the microscope. As long as I'm involved with the team, and while people think we're together, people are going to talk, and watch, and take photos and videos, and who knows what else. Everything I do is going to come under scrutiny because I'm a woman. Everything I do for the team, people will claim it's wrong, that I don't know what I'm doing. Some of the time, that'll be right, but the rest of the time I'll be acting on advice from those who know, or my own business experience. They think I'm going to fuck this up, but I'm not."

"Of course you're not," I said. "Haven't I been trying to tell you that? Maybe I haven't done a good enough job."

"You might have, but I need to tell it to myself," she said. "Because I need faith in myself to get past all the things people are going to say. I need to be able to stand on my own two feet."

"What are you saying?" Why was my heart suddenly in my throat?

"I'm saying that I'm done taking on board all the things people think they know about me," she said. "I'm done listening to opinions that don't matter. I'm done letting gossip and rumors and innuendos make decisions for me. If the Internet wants to talk about me, let them. If they want to suggest I like to practice giving blowjobs to sausages, I don't give a shit anymore. I'm going to do my job and live my life the way I want to."

She looked over at me. Her eyes glittered in the light of dozens of streetlights. "I'm done fighting the way I feel about you. I care about you, Cam. A lot. If people have a problem with that, that's their problem. Not mine, not yours, not ours."

My heart felt like it was sliding across the ice. Heading straight for the basket. With no goalie there to stop it from sliding straight on in.

"I care about you too, Andi Welling," I whispered. "Welcome to the world of not giving a shit about what social media says. I'm sure my sister Alice will have a lot to say about it to both of us. Probably something along the lines of taking control of the narrative."

"That sounds about right," Andi said reluctantly. "I guess I'll have to come out and admit I like to eat sausages."

My balls were suddenly twice as heavy.

I grinned. "I can see a hotdog eating session in my future. Possibly with the whole team." That was very much something Alice would suggest. Reminding people that there was no need to sexualize eating anything. Except pussy, which I very much wanted to taste right now.

I leaned in and brushed my lips over Andi's.

"You should be downstairs, playing," she said against my mouth.

I slid my hand higher up her thigh. "If you insist."

She laughed. "That wasn't what I meant." But she wasn't pushing me away either.

I took the plate from her and set it aside before wrapping my arms around her and pulling her until she was straddling my lap, facing me. My steadily growing erection was nestled right between the juncture of her thighs.

"I don't think Coach is expecting me back too

soon." I rolled my hips, rubbing my cock against her pussy, only our clothes between us.

"What is the boss expecting?" Her voice was already breathless. She pressed herself against me, grinding lightly.

"To feel good," I said firmly. I kissed her again, more deeply this time, my hand on the back of her head, fingers tangled in her glorious hair. "You deserve to feel good."

"You make me feel good." Her hands were pressed against my chest, one right over my heart.

I slid one of my hands up the front of her sweater —blue this time, with the Sea Dragons logo, Ceecee on the front—and rubbed my thumb over her pebbled nipple.

She moaned softly. "Cam... If you keep doing that I'm going to..."

"Do it," I whispered. "Come for me. I want to hear you."

"Cam," she whimpered my name and ground herself harder against me. "Oh my goodness, I—"

She came apart right there, in my lap, rubbing her clit against my hardened cock. Her breath was a series of tiny little gasps and moans that were almost enough to make me lose my load in my shorts.

I barely managed to hang on until she was done,

before rubbing her nipple a couple more times and kissing her delicious mouth.

"Now I can concentrate on playing," I said. "After giving you that. The first of many." I was certain of that. I wanted to take her in every possible way.

"But you didn't." She glanced down at my shorts.

"Not yet," I said. "That's something to look forward to." I kissed her mouth and thought unsexy thoughts as I helped her to her feet.

Hand in hand, we started back down to join the rest of the world.

Chapter Nineteen

Andi

Back straight, I stepped through the door, into the team box.

Like nothing happened, I sat back down beside my mother, but not before scooping up a large cupcake on the way past. A chocolate one, with decorative chocolate frosting. Exactly the kind that would horrify her.

She glanced over at me, eyes widening as I licked frosting of the side.

"Yes, I am going to eat this," I said. "And I'm going to enjoy every mouthful. Are you going to watch me eat it?"

"Why would I watch you eat?" she asked tersely.

"It seems like the latest Lowball Bay pastime," I

said. "And you've made a fine art out of it for the last thirty years."

"That wasn't what I meant when I said you should watch what you eat." She looked away from my cupcake and her expression softened. "Are you okay? I was worried about you. When I saw that you couldn't breathe... I didn't know what to do."

"I'm fine," I said lightly. "It's going to take more than a piece of Frank to take me down. Although, I should thank whoever dislodged it for me."

"It was her." Cynthia nodded to a woman who stood behind us. She was about my age, slender with pale pink hair.

She smiled shyly at me.

I smiled back. "Thank you. If you hadn't thought so quickly, I might not be here now."

She shrugged. "I acted without thinking, but you're welcome. Gotta be careful of those hotdogs." She winked and smiled warmly. She looked vaguely familiar, but I couldn't quite place her.

"That's what I keep telling Andrea," Cynthia said.

"If you told me I might choke on one and almost die, I might have avoided them," I said.

"I think what I said was that if you keep eating

that rubbish, it'll kill you," she eyed the cupcake again. "So technically, I was correct."

"Life is too short not to eat cake." I bit into the side of mine. "What's the score?"

Fully aware she wouldn't have a clue, I glanced over at the scoreboard.

In the first few minutes of the third period, the Sea Dragons were leading two goals to one.

I'd missed most of the game while I hid in my office, and then dry humped Cam until I had an orgasm in his lap.

What came over me? I'd never done that with anyone before. But Cam and I, we fit together so perfectly. His touch had sent electricity rocketing all the way through me. And his cock, his cock felt so big. So perfect rubbing against my clit. I wanted more. I wanted to know how he'd feel inside me.

Was my face pink now? Probably; it was warm. I kept it hidden as best I could behind my cupcake and told my clit to calm down for now. Later, she could come out again and play.

She seemed happy with that, for now.

"I have no idea what's going on," Cynthia admitted. "It seems to involve a lot of pushing and shoving, with the occasional use of the stick against that little rubber thing." She waved her hand vaguely, but the sides of her mouth hinted at a smile. She wasn't as oblivious as she let on.

I couldn't help laughing. "It's called a puck, Mom. The idea is to get that into the goal. Preferably without getting punched in the face, or losing teeth."

She looked horrified, in a fascinated kind of way. "Barbaric." She wouldn't let on, but she was actually enjoying the game.

"That's what we like about it," the pink-haired woman said from behind us.

Cynthia clicked her tongue.

I ignored her and followed Cam around the ice with my gaze. He seemed to be everywhere, all at once. On and off as they switched back and forth between him and another winger. I didn't know how they kept track of shifts, but no one missed a beat, switching out quickly every forty-five seconds or so.

I cheered as Blake stopped a goal with his glove at the last moment, preventing the Tornadoes from equaling the score. Moments later, Cam had posses-sion of the puck and slapped it over to the right winger, who slapped it back before Cam flicked it past the opposition's goalie and into the basket.

I found myself on my feet, cheering and clapping along with everyone else.

He turned his face and looked straight at me

before raising his stick to point in my direction. He nodded and grinned.

That goal was for me.

The crowd went wild and, once again I was on the big screen, this time grinning proudly, rather than choking. Hopefully this was the footage that went viral, not the hotdog. Yeah, that was a faint hope, but a girl could dream, couldn't she?

"I assume that was a good thing," my mother said. "The score seems to be three to one in our favor."

I sat back down and raised my eyebrows at her. "It's *ours* now, is it?" I half-teased.

"My daughter owns the team, therefore it's ours," she said with a sniff. "I suppose you expect me to attend more games."

"I don't expect anything, Mom," I said gently. "But if you'd like to join me, I'll be happy to have you here. Dad too. You should try a cupcake. These are really good." I finished the last of mine and licked frosting from my fingers. "I realized something from almost choking to death. Life is too short not to enjoy every moment of it. If that means having a treat once in a while, then where's the harm?"

Predictably, she looked unconvinced. "I brought a banana." She reached into her bag.

"I'll remember to have catering supply bananas next time," I assured her. If my mother wanted bananas, then bananas she should have.

"Be careful eating that though. Especially if the camera is turned in our direction." That did *not* need to go viral. I didn't know who'd be more horrified, her or me.

Pia would find the whole thing hilarious. Hotdog, banana, whatever. She'd be rolling on the floor laughing at the sight of it. Except the bit where I almost died. The fact she wasn't blowing up my phone with text messages meant she hadn't seen it yet. She would, soon enough.

"I know you think I'm a boring old lady," Cynthia started. "but I just want you to live a long, healthy life. Is that so terrible?"

"Not at all." I was surprised she hadn't added 'productive,' but for once, she didn't. Maybe she was lightening up. "It just means you care. But I don't need a lecture. Or to be judged. Not from you. Just support me and cheer me on. And I'll do the same to you. In fact, I think we should work together to organize a charity event. We can get the whole team involved."

Briefly I wondered if we could incorporate the

team hotdog eating session, but I suspected that might be a step too far for my mother.

"I'd enjoy that, Andrea," she said.

"Andi," I corrected.

She lowered her eyebrows slightly and went on eating her banana.

One step at a time.

I returned my attention to the ice as the fourth period began.

By the time the horn sounded at the end of the game, even my mother was on her feet, clapping and smiling. She didn't cheer, but this was enough. Seeing her enjoy herself, and her appreciation for the team, made my heart a little happier. A little lighter.

Did she have any idea how much it meant to me that we were sharing this? That she wasn't just sitting in her chair, her arms crossed, looking like she wanted to be anywhere but here?

No, that pose was usually reserved for things like school plays and piano recitals. She valued the arts, she even raised money for it, but she didn't want her daughters in occupations that could be considered artistic. As far as she was concerned, that wasn't real work. Even after seeing me practice piano for hours at a time. Making her proud was always one of my biggest challenges.

Tonight, I felt like maybe I was capable of doing just that.

Cam and the rest of the team were skating around, hugging each other and grinning. And shaking hands with opposition players as they skated past. Making me proud was something he did effortlessly. Not only because I owned the team, but because I was learning to appreciate the game and the skill it took to do what he did. He made it look easy, but it was far from it.

And that was hot as hell.

He looked up at me and waved, smiling bigger than I'd seen him do before. If he wasn't careful, he'd lose his reputation as the team grump.

His smile faded when Nate shouldered him, shoving him back a couple of feet. He looked as though he might take a swing at the other player, but shook his head and shoved him back with his hands.

"That's the man who kissed you," Cynthia said. "Isn't it? What's going on between you two? He came in here looking for you. He seemed very angry and concerned." Her expression was cautious.

"We care about each other," I said.

If she knew what we did on the couch in my office, her expression would be more than cautious.

"I'm not sure where it'll go."

The whole thing was so new, I hadn't had time to spare a thought for the future. Did we have one? I liked him a lot, but what if my schedule was too much for him? What if he, like Xander, decided I was too busy and distant? Not to mention how busy he was with training, traveling and playing.

Caring about each other was one thing, making it work was another.

"He's not your usual type," she pointed out.

"You mean he doesn't wear a suit to work," I said. "A suit is just a different kind of uniform."

She sniffed. "A perfectly tailored suit is completely different to," she gestured down to the ice, "a sporting uniform. How long can he expect to keep doing this? What is he going to do after that? Does he have any other skills for a job that doesn't involve skating and punching?"

"I don't know, Mom. Maybe he's going to retire and sit on the beach all day counting the grains of sand." He'd be bored in about six seconds.

"There's no need to be sarcastic, Andrea," she said.

Apparently whatever headway we made was as far as we were going to get tonight.

"I'm concerned for you and your future. Don't jump in blind and then regret it because you didn't ask the right questions."

"This isn't a corporate merger, or a hostile takeover," I said.

"No, it might be the rest of your life," she said.

She let out a long, weary sigh. Like somehow she was disappointed in my lack of ability to appreciate her point of view.

Correction, my lack of willingness to appreciate her telling me what to do and judging every little thing. My lack of cooperation in behaving exactly the way she expected me to, moment by moment.

I must be very fucking disappointing to her.

"It seems the game is over, you can drive me home." And that was the end of the conversation as far as she was concerned.

"Okay, Mom." I grabbed up my things and followed her out the door.

Before it closed behind me, I managed to send off a quick text.

Chapter Twenty

Cam

Blake flopped into the seat beside me, his head cocked, gaze full of scrutiny.

"What?" He looked at me like I had something on my face. I kept my hands on my thighs. Knowing him he was trying to stir something up. I refused to bite.

"There's something different about you," he said. His gaze dropped to my chin, then rose to the top of my head before returning to my eyes. He tipped his head from side to side and tried not to smile too big.

"Sure there is." I grabbed my seatbelt and clicked the two sides together before adjusting it across my lap.

That wasn't an end to the conversation, but he

wasn't going to reel me in. Whatever he had to say, he'd get to it sooner or later. Preferably sooner.

The goalie couldn't resist making a joke out of anything and everything. I'd lost count of how many times I told him he should have been a clown or a comedian. Apparently those options were his backup plans if hockey didn't work out.

Nate would have suggested he had too many pucks to the head. Blake would have been faster to agree with him than I would. He didn't take himself seriously either. Once in a while, I almost envied him. Nothing got to him for long. Everything got to me more than it should.

"No, there is." He fastened his own seatbelt. "You took off from the ice and came back looking like the donkey that got the carrot." He squinted. "That's it, isn't it?"

"Yes, I ran off to eat a carrot and now my life is complete," I said sarcastically.

"I knew there was something weird about you," he said with a laugh. "If a carrot is all it takes to make you happy, you could have had one years ago."

"Are you going to be weird the entire flight? Because if you are, go and sit next to someone else. Seattle is too far to deal with whatever happy pills you took."

He grinned. "I'm not the one who took happy pills. Or a happy carrot. Or are we talking about a carrot top?" His expression became sly.

I suppressed the very strong urge to smile at the thought of Andi and her gorgeous red curls. Nothing would give the game away faster than a silly grin like a kid with a crush.

Instead, I went with playing it casual.

"I think describing someone with red hair as a carrot top might be considered offensive." I pressed on the screen in front of me, hoping to find a good movie to watch.

Honestly, I would have preferred to spend the flight looking at Andi. After making her come like that, I hadn't been able to get her out of my mind.

She was the first thing I thought of when I woke up in the morning and the last thing on my mind before I went to sleep. And pretty much everything in between. All I wanted to do was see her and talk to her. Wrap my arms around her and bury myself inside her. Taste her until she screamed my name.

We'd barely had time to exchange text messages before the whole team was off to the airport to fly out. Usually, I enjoyed traveling, but this time I would have preferred to stay home.

"Flynn, do you get offended when anyone calls

you carrot top?" Blake shouted out through the plane.

Flynn turned around in his seat, gave Blake a funny look and turned back to his conversation with Nate, who sat beside him.

Blake shrugged and checked his seatbelt. "I guess he doesn't care too much."

"Flynn isn't easily offended," I pointed out.

"That's true," Blake conceded. "That's it though, right? You took off after Andi, and something happened between you." He looked as though he'd made up his mind, regardless of whatever I told him. I could deny it flat and he'd still be convinced he was right.

"It might have," I said. This conversation was inevitable, but that didn't mean I had to enjoy it.

"Bro." Blake held out his fist for a bump.

Sighing reluctantly, I bumped my fist against his.

"Is she okay?" Blake asked.

"Because she's into me?" I frowned. If he was going to start insulting her, we were going to have a problem, even if he was only doing it to tease. No one said anything negative about her in front of me and got away with it.

"Because she almost choked," he said, clearly amused at my response.

Okay, I'd put two and two together and came up with six. But after the things I'd seen about her online, I couldn't help being protective. Did she need me to be? Maybe not. Was I going to be protective anyway? Yeah, yeah I was. If anyone was going to be a dick to her, they could go through me.

"Right," I said into my chest. "Yeah, she's okay. A bit shaken, and a lot embarrassed. It's not everyday shit like that happens in front of a bunch of people. Alice said no one wants to run with that footage. Apparently it's too distressing for sensitive viewers."

It was fucking distressing to me. I doubted Andi wanted to see it either.

"And if you mention anything about sausages or licking cupcakes, I will rearrange your face," I said.

He held up his hands in surrender. "I wasn't going to say a word. I like Andi, I think she's good for the team. She's clearly good for you."

"Yes, she is," I said, agreeing with both points. "She's genuine. Real."

"Is she the jealous kind, and does she know about the carrot?" Blake grinned.

"You're an idiot," I told him. "If you're so into carrots, I'll give you their phone number. Or better yet, buy you a packet of them when we land."

"No offense, but I prefer brunettes," he said.

"Hey, maybe that's what's wrong with Zack." He spoke loud enough to be heard a few rows ahead of us.

"He needs a carrot?" I asked.

"I was going to say he has one up his ass, but that works too," Blake said.

"Fuck off," Zack called back. "I don't screw vegetables. Stop projecting, Eastwood."

Blake grinned. "I don't know, it feels like I touched a nerve."

"You're getting on my last nerve," Zack said.

"Settle down," Coach Lambton called out.

The flight attendants secured the cabin and the plane engine roared to life. Moments later, we were taxiing down the runway and heading up into the sky.

"Is she traveling with us, or does she have a private jet?" Blake asked.

"She has work to do." I'd hoped she could accompany us, but from her text messages, she just started digging through everything she needed to know about the team.

Besides, this thing between us was still new. We had to figure out whether we could work together and date, and not let those two things interfere with each other. What would happen if we couldn't keep them separate? I wasn't giving her up, and I wasn't ready to retire yet.

"I guess you brought a spare carrot then?" Blake ducked away when I went to sock him on the arm.

"I don't need a carrot, much less a spare one," I said. "I'm not cheating on her with a carrot. Or anything else for that matter."

"Not even a strawberry?" He pretended to look serious. It lasted all of several seconds.

I shook my head. "I don't even know how anyone would sleep with a strawberry."

This wasn't even the strangest conversation I'd ever had with one of my teammates. Just the strangest one today.

"Seems like you've given the matter a lot of thought." He grinned.

"It seems like you've given it much more thought than anyone else," I retorted. "Look, I'm not going to judge you for your preference."

He grinned wider. "Yes you are."

"Okay, if you wanted to get intimate with fruit, I would totally judge you. Better you put your dick in a salad bowl than my sister."

I trusted her judgment, but I knew what my teammates were like. Guys like Nate, and Blake, they weren't the kind to stick around. I didn't want to have to pick up the pieces after they broke her heart. Or after she broke their nose for being assholes to her.

I really, really didn't want to have to break their noses on her behalf. That shit was not good for team morale.

"She is cute," Blake said thoughtfully.

I narrowed my eyes at him and growled, "Don't go there. That goes for all the guys on the team. If any of you mess with her, they'll regret it."

His response was to flash me a smile and tap the screen in front of him to turn on a different movie.

I gave him a last glance before pushing my earbuds into my ears and settling back to enjoy the flight.

CAM

Hey, gorgeous

I thought about writing something else, something more, but sent the text off anyway.

A dot appeared, showing Andi read my message. Three dots bounced across the left side of the screen before her response popped up.

ANDI

Hey, handsome.

Yes, she used a period.

CAM

How's things there on the east coast? 🦆

ANDI

Cold but quiet. 🥶

CAM

Missing me?

I smiled at my phone, while picturing her looking at hers, reading my messages.

ANDI

Which one are you again? 😏😏

CAM

You know how to hurt a guy. 🙂

ANDI

ANDI

I know who you are. You're the guy with the killer dimples.

CAM

And you're the woman who looks amazing when she 

ANDI

ANDI

I've been thinking about the other night.

CAM

Me too. What are you wearing?

ANDI

ANDI

Who says I'm wearing anything?

Hello, my cock stood up to take notice.

CAM

I'm alone in my hotel room if you want to show me

My heart raced. I didn't expect her to send me nude photos, but hell, if she wanted to, I was here for it.

The dots bounced again before a photo popped up. It showed a bare, freckled shoulder.

CAM

> Can I lick those freckles when I get back to Lowball Bay?

ANDI

ANDI

Maybe.

Another photo popped up, this time of the side of her face, from an awkward angle. The bottom of the photo barely showed the top of her mouth, curved up in a smile.

ANDI

I suck at selfies.

ANDI

CAM

> You do not suck at selfies. You're beautiful

To show her I was at least as bad, I took a photo of the top of my head and sent it to her.

ANDI

ANDI

> I want to run my fingers through that.

Now I was the one with a heated face.

CAM

> I want to tangle my fingers in your hair and watch you suck my 🍆

ANDI

> I bet you have a delicious 🍆

CAM

> I bet you have a delicious 🐼 I look forward to tasting her when I get home

Three dots bounced, then stopped, then bounced again. Had I gone too far? I didn't want to push her into anything she wasn't ready for, including texting like this. I was about to type an apology when her response popped up.

ANDI

> I'd like that.

I grinned.

CAM

I have to go and warm up for tonight's game. We're flying out late, right after, heading to Vancouver. Then we'll be home again

ANDI

ANDI

I miss you.

CAM

See you in a couple of days, beautiful.

Chapter Twenty-One

Andi

A SOFT TAP ON MY DOOR WOKE ME FROM MY doze. I sat up and blinked a couple of times, glancing at the time on the microwave. I must have fallen asleep in front of the TV, a blanket draped over myself. So much for leaving it on to keep me awake.

The tap sounded again, as soft as the first time. Tentative. Not like the man doing the tapping.

I shoved the blanket off myself and managed to stand without tangling my feet in it.

Bonus.

Now, if I could make it all the way to the door without mishap, I might be winning against the universe for a while.

Mindful the universe might be vengeful if she heard me thinking like this, I moved carefully and undid the two chains and three locks on my door before pulling it open.

"Hi." Seeing Cam standing outside my apartment, looking gorgeous with a few days' worth of growth on his chin, I was suddenly shy.

"Can I come in?" He tilted his head far enough to peer through the gap with both eyes.

"Right, of course." I stepped back, drawing the door with me.

"You look beautiful." He leaned over to kiss me before walking into my apartment.

"No, you," I said automatically. Great, now he probably thought I lost my mind. I closed the door and locked it behind him.

He turned around and raised his eyebrows. "I don't think anyone's called me beautiful before." He took my hands and pulled me to his chest.

"Why wouldn't they?" I raised my chin to look up at him. He was a few inches taller than me when I wasn't wearing heels. "It's true."

"You're the beautiful one." He pressed the tip of his nose to mine. "I missed you. I haven't been able to get you out of my head. Either of them."

I felt the second one growing as he pressed it against me.

"Me either," I whispered. "I mean, I only have one head. I mean... Shit."

Good job, Andi. I was as smooth as crunchy peanut butter.

He chuckled, his breath warm on my face. "You have one gorgeous head." He wrapped his arms around me, and slid his hands down to cup my rear. "And the cutest ass on the entire East Coast."

"Now that's where you're wrong," I said. I reached around to cup his. "This is the cutest ass in the country."

"Hmmm, I'm afraid I'm going to have to contradict you," he said. "There's absolutely no ass cuter than yours."

"Cameron North, if you're going to contradict the boss, we might have a problem," I teased.

"Are you going to punish me?" he asked.

If my pulse wasn't racing before, it was now.

"I might, but we could also come to some kind of compromise," I said. "We can agree that yours is the cutest ass on any man in the country."

I arched a brow expectantly.

"I think you're hoping I'll say yours is the cutest ass on any woman in the country," he said slowly. "But I stand by what I said. Yours is much cuter." He gripped me tighter and picked me up until I wrapped my legs around his waist. His mouth met mine in a kiss that should have set the apartment on fire.

He carried me over to the couch and lay me down, before lying over me, his knees on either side of my thighs.

"I've been thinking about this for days," he whispered. "Kissing you. Being with you." He kissed me again, then pulled away and frowned. "Unless you just wanted to talk?"

"No," I said. "Yes. I mean, I want to talk, but I want to kiss you first. Unless you want to talk?"

"I want to have a long bath and a conversation with you, after I taste your pussy and make you come," he said. "Is that too direct?"

"No, no," I said quickly. "That's exactly direct enough. Don't stop." I wrapped my arms around the back of his neck and pulled his face down so I could kiss his mouth and trace my lips over his.

He ran his hands up and down my body, touching me everywhere, only layers of clothes between us.

He kissed my mouth, down my cheek and my neck. The more he kissed me, the more I wanted. The more I needed.

"Please," I whispered.

"Please, what?" he asked, his face buried close to my throat. "Tell me what you need."

"Everything," I said.

He pushed himself up and propped himself on his elbow to look down at me. "Everything? You might need to elaborate."

I grabbed the front of his shirt and pulled him back down to me to kiss him more thoroughly. I let my hands wander up his shirt and across his muscular back. Holy puck, it felt like his muscles had muscles.

That thought promptly made me feel self-conscious. My hands and mouth went still, frozen, wondering what the hell a guy like this was doing with me.

He lifted his head and frowned. "What is it? Do you want to stop?" He rolled off me and knelt on the floor beside the couch. His eyes were dark with desire, but laced with worry. "Andi, speak to me. What is it?"

"No," I said softly. "It's not you. It's one hundred percent me." I sighed out my nose in frustration.

He pushed himself off the floor to sit beside me and hold both of my hands. "You're beautiful. You know that, right?"

I shook my head sadly. "I don't know that. I

mean, I believe you believe that, but I don't see it when I look in the mirror. I see crazy hair I can't control, too many freckles and..." I gestured down at myself.

"The most incredible body I've ever seen," he said firmly. "Is that what this is about? You think I'll judge you because other people do? Firstly, I wouldn't do that, because you're stunning. Secondly, fuck them for making you feel bad about yourself. When I look at you, I see a smart, gorgeous, intelligent, caring person. Someone who's probably too good for a dork like me."

"You're not a dork," I insisted. "You're gorgeous and sexy. You deserve a woman who doesn't look at herself and remember the things people say about her. Someone who doesn't eat too many hotdogs and cupcakes."

A flash of anger crossed his features. "Who told you you shouldn't eat whatever you want to?"

"Society as a whole," I whispered, withdrawing slightly from his fury. "My mother in particular. Girls from school. My mirror is a particularly judgemental bitch."

"If that's the case, I'll smash it for you," he offered. "It'll be worth seven years of bad luck." He cupped my cheek with his hand. "I'm sorry people were assholes to you. It's not okay. No one should be treated like that by *anyone*."

He looked as though he wanted to growl at my mother, but understood it was a battle for me and her, not for him to undertake on my behalf.

"No, they shouldn't," I agreed. "I shouldn't let it get to me. I just... I look at you and I... You're out of my league."

"You have that backwards," he said. "You're out of mine. I'm a guy who hits a piece of rubber with a stick. Sure, it entertains people and inspires kids to get up off the couch, put on a pair of skates and have some fun, but..."

"You work hard, and yes, you are a role model, which is important. You're making a difference. I sit in an office making decisions that are designed to make people more money. How is that useful?" I sighed softly.

"I heard about the charity event you're organizing," he said. "What could be *more* useful? I tell you what, we're both making a difference in the world, we're just doing it in different ways. But you, you look good doing it." He leaned over and kissed my forehead.

"So do you," I said.

He put an arm around me and pulled me to him.

"When was the last time anyone made you feel special?"

"I don't know," I admitted. "My..."

Now would be a good time to tell him about Xander. Cam would find out sooner or later. Better he hear it from me than some other source. Especially if that source was the always unreliable world wide web. Who knew what stories were circulating about my previous relationship?

I didn't want to look it up. Xander was firmly in the past, where he belonged.

"My last boyfriend lived here, up until a few months ago." It felt like several lifetimes. Every time I was with Cam, I felt more alive than ever before. More real. He made me want to be a better person, one who embraces every day and all the challenges that come with existing. Not just existing, but really *living*.

"His idea of 'special' was putting his coffee cup in the dishwasher." Xander knew it annoyed me when he left it on the countertop and walked away. I'd glared at him a few times before he cottoned on to my irritation. He rolled his eyes, but he hadn't done it since.

"And having his assistant message me to tell me

he'd be home late. And I did the same to him," I said quickly, before Cam judged him too harshly.

"Sometimes, I think he had a better relationship with Rafe than he did with me." Rafe could have told me what Xander wanted for Christmas, his birthday or an anniversary present. I suspected that went both ways, that Xander got his ideas about gifts for me, from Rafe.

No one else would have suggested he buy me a life-size cardboard cutout of Damon Salvatore, and he wouldn't have figured it out for himself. The cutout sat in front of the window in my home office.

If you're wondering, yes he was better company than Xander. He had a lot more personality. And was always smiling at me.

"Then he wasn't trying hard enough," Cam concluded. "I'm going to make you feel so special, the next time we get hot and bothered together you won't second-guess yourself and the way I feel about you."

"You don't want to..." Of course he didn't. Why would he?

In spite of my insecurities, I knew that wasn't what he was saying. What he really meant was something much deeper than our physical attraction. Something more important.

He placed his hands on my cheeks and turned

my face to him. "I want to fuck you more than I've ever wanted anyone else." He hesitated for a moment, and shook his head.

"No, I want to *make love* to you. If that means waiting until you understand that's what it is, then that's what I'll do." He lightly kissed my mouth. "When the time comes, it'll be worth every second of the wait. Because you're worth it."

I swallowed down a knot of emotion that threatened to bring tears to my eyes again. This time, not tears of humiliation, but ones of warmth like nothing I'd felt before. The potential of something mind-blowingly amazing.

Was there a hint of doubt in my mind because he was still a smoking hot hockey god? Yes, but I understood he wanted to help me to see myself the way he did.

That was...everything.

"I want that too," I said. I wanted to feel him everywhere, but he was right. Whatever this was growing between us, it was different.

We might have a lifetime together, but the stronger we build the foundation, the better chance we had of weathering the storms that were thrown at us.

Chapter Twenty-Two

Cam

I placed the bag of groceries down on the kitchen island and turned to watch Andi.

She'd tied her hair back into a ball of red curls. Some of it had snuck out of her hair tie and sprang up to frame her face. The freckles on her nose stood out, illuminated by the sun slanting in as she stopped to look out at the ocean.

"I didn't realise you lived so close by." She turned slowly to face me.

"Walking distance." I started to pull the groceries out of the bag. Flour, eggs, milk, butter, cocoa powder, sugar. Everything the recipe listed.

"Convenient." She smiled.

"We could carpool." I grabbed out a bowl and spoon.

"You're usually there earlier than I am," she said. "You cook?"

"I don't just cook," I said, picking up the flour to start measuring the right amount. "I can bake." I waved the spoon in the air like a flourish, and bowed.

"Impressive." She stepped over and leaned her hip against the side of the island.

"Don't be too impressed, I haven't baked in years. Not since I helped my mother make birthday cakes. This could all go horribly wrong."

"I can't bake at all. That may increase the odds of this being an absolute disaster." She picked up my tablet and read the recipe. "Chocolate cupcakes?"

"I heard a rumor you like them," I said. "I figured it was something we could do together." I'd racked my brains, trying to think of something special I could do for her and came up with a list. This was the first item of many.

"Okay, where do we start?" she asked.

I glanced over at the recipe. "It says we have to cream the butter and sugar."

I frowned and thought back. "I think that means we have to mix them together until they look creamy." I measured the butter and put it into the bowl with the sugar, but then tapped at the butter with the spoon. It was cold and hard.

"This might take a while." I picked up the bowl, tucked it into my elbow and started trying to stir the mixture. I gritted my teeth and worked at it until it finally started to soften. "This might be harder than playing hockey."

"It certainly looks like it," she agreed. "It says we have to sift the flour next. What does that mean?"

I peered over at the recipe. "I don't know. I guess we can just throw it into the bowl."

I placed the bowl on the countertop and picked up the flour. The bottom of the bag broke, sending flour pouring down onto the black marble, and flying into the air like a puff of smoke.

"Shit." I waved a hand in front of myself to clear the air. All I succeeded in doing was turning my hand white and scattering the flour even further. "That wasn't supposed to happen."

Andi giggled. "I didn't think it was. Is there enough left in the bag for the cupcakes?"

I held up the bag in front of me and peered into one end. The end that was supposed to be open. I raised it higher and looked at her through the empty paper bag.

"Nope." Flour was everywhere except where it was supposed to be. All over the island and drifting down to the floor. The front of my shirt was covered in it. My jeans too.

"I don't suppose we can bake a cake without it," she said.

"Probably not," I agreed, my smile growing playfully sly. "But we can do this." I grabbed up two handfuls of flour and threw them at her. The fine powder hit her in the chest and chin, covering her skin and purple sweater.

For a moment, I thought she'd be angry. I cursed myself for acting so rash. She might walk right out the door and never speak to me again.

But then, she laughed and scooped up more of the flour to flick at me.

"Like that, is it?" I grinned. "You wanted a war? You've got one." With the back of my hand, I scraped a pile of flour to the edge of the island and swept it in her direction.

She squealed and waved her hands in front of her face. "You suck." But she was laughing and flicking flour back at me.

I picked up a couple of handfuls and stalked her around the island, while she tried to evade me.

"You can run, but you can't hide." I grinned. I followed her around to the original pile of flour before realizing she'd drawn me there so she could grab up more and throw it at me. I ducked and threw mine at her legs.

I was laughing so hard, I wasn't paying attention to where I was going. I slipped on a pile of flour. Windmilling my arms, I lost my balance and fell on my ass.

She grabbed something off the counter and disappeared behind the island.

I wasn't sure where she was or what she was up to, until she appeared right behind me. With a giggle of glee, she cracked an egg directly over my head, the cold contents dribbling onto my hair. She threw the shell in the direction of the trash and bolted to the other side of the kitchen.

I sat on the floor and let the egg trickle down my head and over my face.

"You're really asking for it, you know that." I wiped egg out of my eyes with the back of my hand.

"Yeah? What are you gonna do about it, Mr. North?"

I pushed myself to my feet and picked up the box of cocoa powder while looking right at her. I pushed my thumb under the cardboard and gave it an exaggerated swipe sideways to open it.

She shook her head. "You wouldn't."

I pulled out the bag from inside the box. I tossed

the box onto the island and pinched either side of the bag with my fingers. "Wouldn't I?" I stalked towards her.

"It would be a waste of perfectly good cocoa powder," she argued. She stepped away from me, hands in front of her.

"I'll make a hefty donation to the food bank," I said. Normally, I hated wasting food, but seeing her covered in flour was worth it.

"I will too," she said. "But only if you don't throw it at me."

I cocked my head at her. "You drive a hard bargain, Ms. Welling." I folded the top of the bag and shoved it back into the box. "I guess I could order some cupcakes to be delivered."

"At this point, that seems like a good idea," she agreed. She wiped a hand over her face, but mostly succeeded in smudging the layer of flour, not removing any of it. "And cleaning all of this up."

I glanced around and grimaced. We'd made a hell of a mess, but I didn't regret a moment of it. Seeing her laughing and enjoying herself was totally worth the amount of time it would take to exorcise all of the flour from the kitchen.

I scooped up my phone from the other side of the island. Somehow, it missed the worst of the flour fight. Bringing my head close to hers, I held up the phone in front of us, the camera on our flour-covered faces.

"While we look like this, we might as well go all the way and take a selfie. I promise I won't share it with the world. Unless you want me to. Say 'chocolate cupcakes.'"

She leaned in closer and smiled. "If only my mother could see me now. Chocolate cupcakes!"

I took a couple of pictures and put the phone back down. "I'll get this sorted, if you want to have a shower," I offered.

Not gonna lie, I would have loved to have a shower with her, but I meant what I'd said. I wanted her to be comfortable with herself before I took her to bed.

Was I going to give myself the worst case of blue balls in history? Probably.

Did I care? No. I cared more about her than I did about getting off. She was more important to me than sex. More important than an hour or two of mind blowing and very gratifying intimacy.

I didn't want her for a night or two. I wanted her for the long run.

When I heard her come again, I'd know she was ready and committed. If that meant listening to her in my shower, and imagining her naked and wet, then so be it. I'd put myself through worse.

"Help yourself to whatever you can find in my closet," I added.

She gave me a nervous glance, but stepped carefully towards my bedroom, leaving a trail of flour on the hardwood floor.

A few moments later, I heard the water turn on.

I waited for the protest from my balls and cock, but for once it didn't come. Yes, they throbbed at the idea of her being so close, and bare, but they seemed to understand the necessity of waiting for a while longer. They were more or less content to know it was a 'when' and not an 'if.'

As content as blue balls could be.

"Focus," I told myself. I grabbed up a sponge and started to wipe down the island, before vacuuming quickly and mopping up the last of the mess.

I was just finishing up when she stepped out of my bedroom, dressed in a pair of my track pants and a Sea Dragons sweatshirt. They were both too big for her, but she looked more edible than when she was covered in food.

"You're so fucking gorgeous," I said softly. "Especially wearing my clothes."

She glanced down at herself. "I might have to get

myself one of these sweatshirts. It's so soft and comfortable." She fingered the fabric.

"Keep it," I said. "I have plenty of them. And I just happen to know a place where I could get more."

Like the rest of the team, I had a closet full of Sea Dragons merchandise, from sweatshirts, to T-shirts, track pants and even socks. Not to mention several caps in various colors. Wherever we went, we were a walking endorsement for our team.

"Me too," she said. "But they don't offer very much in green. I might have to talk to someone about that."

"That's a terrible oversight." I rinsed the sponge under the faucet until it was clear of flour. "I knew the previous owner wasn't doing right by us, but I had no idea how deep it went."

She laughed. "I don't think it was all bad. The team is a good one, we just need to tweak a few things. Hiring your sister was the start of that. I also want to bring in some more trainers for gym work-outs. For other staff as well as the players. And replace the broken equipment in there."

"We'd appreciate that," I said. "Having to share three treadmills when the other three don't work kinda sucks."

She frowned. "How long have they not worked?"

I shrugged. "As long as I've been with the team. We're used to it by now."

"You shouldn't have to be," she said. "I'll get onto that. And finding somewhere for a daycare. That should have been a thing a long time ago too."

"The staff will love that," I agreed. Now I was picturing us both dropping off our kids in the daycare, while we went to work in other parts of the building.

One thing at a time, I told myself.

"I've ordered cupcakes and pizza," I said. "They should be here right after I have a shower. Make yourself comfortable." I waved at the sectional in front of the huge projector screen.

Her being here, in my apartment, felt right. Like she lived here already. I wanted her to. I wanted to wake up to her every morning, and hold her in my arms every night.

I didn't know when it happened, but I'd fallen in love with Andi Welling.

Chapter Twenty-Three

Andi

"You two are so cute together," Rafe whispered loudly as he opened the door to let Cam and me inside. "It's about time too. I've been shipping both of you since, I don't know, it feels like forever." He waved his hand vaguely and closed the door behind us.

I turned my face to speak over my shoulder to Cam. "I think he means a week or two."

"Don't make me kick you out," Rafe said. He rolled his eyes playfully and gestured towards the media room at the back of his and Jacoby's apartment.

"He wouldn't dare," I said to Cam.

"I would dare," Rafe retorted. "But we've been looking forward to your company, right Jacoby?"

"Absolutely." Jacoby rolled past us in his wheel-chair and stopped in his favorite spot near the front of the room. On his lap, he had two big bowls of popcorn. One of which he handed to me and the other to Rafe. To Cam, he offered his hand. "Nice to meet you. Rafe's told me you're a decent guy."

Cam shook his hand and smiled. "I like to think I'm decent."

"What Jacoby means is we both watch out for Andi," Rafe said. "If we didn't think you were good enough for her, we wouldn't have invited you here tonight." He placed his bowl of popcorn down and grabbed a few bottles of beer out of the fridge at the side of the room.

"It's good to know people have her back." Cam accepted a beer and slid into a seat. "If I wasn't good enough for her, I wouldn't have come."

Rafe snorted.

Jacoby grinned. "I appreciate a man who has confidence in himself," the dark-haired man said. "It's one of the things I like the most about Rafe. He knows who he is and he doesn't give a shit what anyone else thinks."

"Hell yeah, I don't," Rafe held up his beer to toast us. "The day you open the window and let your last fuck fly free, is the best day ever."

Maybe I should try to open a few more windows. I had too many fucks still living in captivity. It was time I let them go, to be the wild fucks they were always meant to be. The worst thing humans ever did was try to domesticate the fuck. Poor things deserved to be out there, living their best lives. Not hanging around our necks like a dead weight.

"I know I promised a *Star Trek* marathon," Rafe said, "So I can educate you Philistines. But Jacoby and I got to talking and we decided on something else."

"Let me guess, we're going to binge watch *Buying Beverly Hills?*" I guessed.

"Nooo." Rafe drew out the word. "Although, I'd happily call the boss 'Daddy' any time." He fanned himself.

"He is a snack," Jacoby agreed. "But we decided on a binge watch of the *Lord of the Rings* movies."

I glanced over at Cam, curious about his reaction.

He glanced back at me. The look in his brown eyes made my pulse race like crazy. "Works for me. As long as Andi is good with that?"

"I'm definitely good with it," I agreed. "I like all things nerdy."

He nodded and draped an arm over the back of

the couch, behind my shoulders. "Me too. Especially if I get to do it with you." He leaned in to kiss my cheek.

"Swoon!" Rafe said happily. "You're both just too fucking adorable." He nudged Jacoby with his elbow. "Aren't they just?"

"Almost as adorable as us," Jacoby agreed. "That happens to be a very high yardstick, by the way. Given Rafe and I are cuter than a basket of kittens."

"I'm not sure if anything is cuter than a basket of kittens, but you're very cute," I replied.

Should it have felt strange to sit here with Cam, Rafe and Jacoby? Xander never came to our binge nights. He always made himself busy instead. Or had a convenient headache.

Being here with Cam felt natural, like we'd done it a million times before. Rafe and Jacoby were excellent judges of character, and if they liked him, maybe I could start to surrender to the feelings that were getting more and more difficult to fight.

Rafe picked up the remote and started the first movie.

I settled back against my seat and into Cam's side. He smelled of soap, and shampoo, and a subtle cologne that had my clit sniffing the air. If he was food, I would have gobbled him up in a couple of bites.

Instead, I dug into the bowl of popcorn, topped with butter and salt, and snacked on that.

"This feels good," he whispered in my ear. "I like being here with you. With my...girlfriend?"

The last word was spoken so softly I wasn't sure if I heard it at all. Girlfriend? Was that what I was? I liked the sound of it.

My heart fluttering, I said, "It's nice to be here with my boyfriend."

When we first met, he seemed to hate my guts at first sight. I would never, in my wildest dreams, have imagined we'd be here like this. But now we sat snuggled together, sharing popcorn and a movie. With no one but our friends to see or scrutinize. No phones to catch us kissing, no big screens to share it with the world.

Just a quiet, intimate moment in front of what had to be the biggest television in existence.

Rafe and Jacoby never did anything by halves.

"Boyfriend," Cam whispered. "I like the way that sounds." He kissed my temple.

"I'd suggest you get a room, but it wouldn't be the first time people had sex in here," Rafe said over his shoulder.

I grimaced at the back of his head. "TMI, Rafe."

He looked back and grinned. "Just don't make a mess."

I had no intention of fucking here, in his media room, especially not with both of them present. I did want to make love to Cam someday soon though.

I'd thought about inviting him to share a shower with me the other day at his apartment, but it wasn't the right time. Not even after the fun we had flinging flour at each other.

I'd kept my word, making a large donation to the food bank, to make up for being so wasteful. I also made a note in my calendar to give them regular donations. No one in the world should experience food insecurity. Anything I could do to help eradicate it, I'd do.

I'd already decided the charity gala my mother and I were going to organize would raise donations for various food banks up and down the east coast. I'd ensure every millionaire and billionaire I knew would contribute. It was the least all of us could do to give back to the community that made us who we were. We could do so much more, and we would, I'd make sure of that.

I nestled up against Cam to enjoy the movies and forget about the real world for a while.

"Hey, you still awake?" Cam whispered several hours and three long movies later.

"Mmmm, yeah." I blinked a couple of times and sat up to stretch. The credits were rolling down the screen. "Why? Was I snoring?"

He chuckled. "No, you just seemed really relaxed. I wasn't sure if you were enthralled in the movie, or asleep with your eyes open."

"Enjoying the movie while being half asleep?" I suggested.

I was definitely relaxed. I tried, but I couldn't remember a time when I felt more so. The only thing that existed for the last few hours was Middle Earth and the warmth of Cam's body beside mine.

Rafe and Jacoby were sitting with their heads together, both snoring softly.

"They really are cute," I whispered.

"If any of the guys on the team fell asleep like that..." Cam started. A sly grin was tugging at the corners of his mouth. His eyes shone with mischief that made my heart flutter and melt a little more.

The more I got to know him, the more I realized his grumpy mask was just that, a mask. Underneath that, he was a sweet, playful, fucking gorgeous guy who I was quickly becoming very attached to.

Part of me was terrified, but the rest of me was like a flash mob, dancing and singing with joy. Also like a flash mob, I didn't know where they'd come from, but I was loving every minute of it.

I smiled. "I know where they keep their Sharpies."

I grabbed his hand and led him out of the room and into my friend's kitchen. Like most people, they had a junk drawer they threw all sorts of random things into. Old batteries, several halves of different colored crayons, a few bottle caps, a bright pink dildo, and a sticker that declared, 'Lowball Bay, Ball capital of America.' And a couple of Sharpies.

I handed one to Cam and we crept back to the media room. Sharpie in hand, I knelt in front of Rafe and carefully drew a mustache across his upper lip. The kind that curls elaborately at the ends.

Cam was giving Jacoby a slim mustache, and a matching, triangular beard.

I pulled out my phone and took a quick photo of both of them before pushing it back into my pocket. I'd never share that with the world, but it would give us all a giggle later.

When they washed it all off and forgave us for drawing on them.

"If you're doing what I think you're doing, you're so fucked," Rafe said without opening his eyes.

I giggled and put the top back on the Sharpie before Cam and I sneaked back out of the media room and slipped quietly out of their apartment. We closed the door behind us and ran, hand-in-hand, before either of them could come after us, throwing cold, buttered popcorn at our backs.

We laughed all the way down to the ground floor, in the elevator, and out to Cam's truck.

"Are they really going to be pissed off?" he asked. He didn't appear to be worried.

"No, but they may try to prank us back," I said. "I advise you not to fall asleep in front of either of them. You may end up with your head shaved, or worse."

"That wouldn't be so bad," he said. He ran a hand over his head. "I could use a haircut."

"It's the 'worse' I'd be worried about," I said. "People have been known to drink with them and wake up with a strange tattoo. One time, it looked suspiciously like Rafe's face. To be fair though, that guy deserved it. He changed all of the sugar in their apartment out and replaced it with salt. If Rafe doesn't get his morning coffee, he will plot vengeance until the end of time."

"No offense to him, but I don't want his face tattooed on me." Cam placed his hands on my shoulders and turned me to face him. "I wouldn't mind your face tattooed on me." After hesitating, he added, "Or your name."

His words drove the breath right out of my lungs. They were matched by the look in his eyes. No one ever looked at me like that before. Open, honest and soft. A direct contrast to the man he was out on the ice. That man would swing a punch without thinking twice, but this man was something else.

"Cam..." I whispered.

"Andi, I'm falling in love with you," he said.

I swallowed hard. "I'm falling in love with you too."

Chapter Twenty-Four

Cam

Rafe gave me the side eye as he passed me in the corridor. Fortunately, that side eye came with a faint smile, not a death glare. He definitely had something planned, but he didn't hate my guts.

I offered my fist for a bump, which he looked at doubtfully before bumping his against it and walking away, chin raised.

Nate looked over his shoulder, confusion etched on his features. "What was that about? Isn't he Andi's assistant?"

"Assistant and good friend," I agreed.

I supposed he was my friend now too, in spite of the whole drawing-a-mustache-on-his-face thing. That was definitely going to come back and bite me in the ass. I was ready for it. I'd already checked everything in my locker for confetti or a glitter bomb.

I had a sneaking suspicion, if he went after either of us, it would be me, not Andi. Partly because I couldn't fire him, and partly because the Internet was still talking about her and the hotdog, and our kiss. They hadn't stopped speculating about what was going on between us.

"So why was her friend giving you a fist bump?" Nate asked. He stared at me, before his eyes widened. "Ah. I see. Cameron North is getting down and dirty with the boss. Good for you, bro." He shoved his shoulder into mine.

I shoved him back. "It's not like that. Don't make it sound salacious."

"Why not, I like salaciousness." He grinned.

"We've noticed," Blake said from behind us. "Isn't it your middle name? Nathanial Salacious Southwell?"

"No, it's David, after my father," Nate said. "But you're right, that was a missed opportunity. Maybe I should change my name."

"How about Nathanial Dickhead Southwell?" Zack pushed past us and stepped into the recently renovated staff gym.

Technically, this wasn't for us, but we were

curious and Andi was proud of the space. In my book, that was a good reason to check it out.

"How about Zack Mashed-potato-for-brains Reed?" Nate called out after him. The words were barely out of his mouth when he blinked a couple of times and gaped.

I followed the line of his gaze to a blonde woman in yoga pants and a pale blue crop top. Her hair was pulled into a ponytail which swung back and forth as she walked towards us.

"Hi, I'm Oaklyn," she greeted us cheerfully. "Resident personal trainer for the staff gym."

"Cam." I nodded my greeting.

"I... I..." Nate stammered. His face actually turned red. "I'm—"

I clapped him on the shoulder. "My articulate friend here is Nate. I'd like to say he can usually put a full sentence together, but that wouldn't be the honest truth. The reality is, he's only here because he's pretty."

Nate glared at me. "I can put a sentence together, asshole." He turned to her and gave her one of his best smiles. The kind which melted panties everywhere he went. "It's nice to meet you, Oaklyn. I'd love to hear about what you do here."

The look she gave him was friendly, but she seemed completely unaffected by his charms.

Blake must have come to the same conclusion, because he chuckled. "This is going to be fun to watch."

I shot him a grin. "Sure is." Nate wasn't used to women who didn't fall at his feet. I had a feeling this woman was going to give him a run for his money. He might just have met his match.

Still, she indulged him by showing him around all the new equipment. She explained that she hoped the staff would make use of it, so she could put together fitness programs for those who wanted them.

"Told you Andi would be good for this place," Flynn said softly. "Wasn't long ago that you disagreed."

"I didn't know her then," I protested. "I didn't know she really cared about the team. I thought she was here to mess with us."

"Now you know better," he said. "Has the team been good for her? I've seen the rumors online. Seems to me like no one was talking about her before she started here. Not really. She was a blip on the radar, as they say. Now, she's practically a Lowball Bay celebrity. How does she feel about that?"

"She's taking it in stride," I said. "She doesn't want to let it get to her."

"None of us do," he said. "Doesn't mean it doesn't. Doesn't mean it won't in the future."

I turned to frown at him. "What are you suggesting? You're the one who wanted me to be a go-between, between her and the rest of the team."

"I did," he said. "But things have progressed between you two."

"Jealous?" Blake asked him, sticking his face between us.

"Not jealous, just concerned," Flynn said. "I was there on the ice, watching while everyone else was watching her. I saw how embarrassed she was. She's going to face that every day if you have a relationship with each other. The scrutiny isn't going to stop. It's easy to say you won't let it bother you, but I've seen it bother you in the past. I saw what it did to you when everyone was talking about you and Clio."

"Don't bring her into this," I snapped. "Andi isn't Clio." I could hardly believe I was hearing this from him. I thought he supported me, no matter what. Wasn't that what friends were for?

"No, she's not," Flynn agreed. "Clio wanted the spotlight. She wanted everything that went along with that, good or bad. She wanted people to talk about her and remember her. And all the endorse-ments and shit that followed. Andi doesn't want any of that. Or does she?"

"No, she doesn't," I said. "She wants to do her job and make a difference in the world." I ran a hand over the back of my head.

Was he right?

It was one thing to turn off our phones and pretend no one cared what we did. It was easy to avoid Googling ourselves to see what people were saying. But it was virtually impossible to ignore glances. People taking photos. People talking about you in whispers.

Did I want that for her for the rest of her life? Hell no, no I didn't. Could I keep her from it? I didn't know the answer to that. Chances were, it was no. Not while we were together, anyway. Not while people cared what I did for a living. On and off the ice.

If I retired and went into coaching, people would still talk. And she'd be caught up in that.

"Shit," I said under my breath. "She isn't the only person to have a partner on the team." It was a weak argument, and I knew it.

"She's the only one who *owns* the team," Blake said.

"Do you have to start on me too?" I asked bitterly.

He shrugged. "Just saying. People are going to have a vested interest in both of you. For the record, I think you're cute together."

"Being cute isn't going to make this easier," Flynn said. "Look, I'm not trying to ruin this for you. I want both of you to be happy, you know that. But I want you to think about what being together means for both of you. You might retire and try to disappear off the face of the planet, but because of your connection with her, they're always going to remember you. As long as you're together, people will be watching. You need to figure out if you can handle it or not. And if you can't, then do her a favor and walk away right now. Before she ends up getting her heart broken. Before you get your heart broken." He gave me a nod and followed Nate on his tour of the small gym.

"I hate to say that he's right, but he's right," Blake said. "We've all seen the way you look at her, even when she thinks you're not looking. I've seen you with a dorky grin on your face when she's not around. You've gone from being a grumpy asshole to someone who's almost tolerable."

"Thanks," I said sarcastically. "It feels like you all

prefer the grumpy asshole. Because that's what you'll get if I end it with her."

Was I seriously considering doing that? We'd told each other we were falling for each other not two days ago. I meant every word.

Now, everything Flynn said began to create a whirlpool in my brain. One that threatened to turn everything upside down and spit us both out. Every word rang way too true.

I told her I was doing special things for her, but everything was in private. At my apartment, and at Rafe's. I'd thought about taking her out somewhere, but dismissed the idea. Why? Because I wanted to save her from scrutiny. I didn't want people watching us. Filming us. Getting up in our faces. Sooner or later, we'd have to step out of the shadows. What would happen then?

Shit, I didn't want to think about it.

"You know we love you, even if you're a grumpy asshole," Blake said. "We don't want to see you hurt, that's all."

He scratched his bearded chin and continued. "Some days, I can't decide if we have the best job, or the worst. We get to play hockey, but people think we belong to them. Like they're entitled to insist on selfies and autographs. I like signing breasts as much as the next guy, but when you're out with someone else, it gets a bit, you know, awkward."

"The last time I went out on a date, she left early because people kept coming up to us. It was too much for her. But better to know that on the first date than on our wedding day. Or after a couple of kids. That would have sucked."

He shrugged as though it wasn't as big a deal as it was. As if bringing children into this life was nothing to be worried about. Too many people didn't bother to filter their thoughts where children were concerned.

"Yeah, I guess it would," I said vaguely.

I should have walked away sooner, before we got in as deep as we were. If I ended it with her, it was going to tear me up, but it would be a lot worse if it happened later. She deserved better than that. She deserved to be happy with someone she could walk around in public with. She deserved to have a normal life, without people pointing fingers at her, and insinuating themselves into her day.

She said she could thicken her skin, but when it came down to it, she shouldn't have to. None of us should, but I chose this life, knowing what came with it. She was thrust into it, thrown straight into the deepest end of the fire, where she could either burn, or tiptoe across the coals.

A flare of anger at her father burst up inside me. He must have had some idea of what he was getting her into. But he'd done it anyway. Her mother too. Both of them had let her walk into this, not really understanding the shit that came with it.

No one doubted she was good for the team. If we stayed together, there was a big chance she'd walk away from the Sea Dragons. To put some sort of distance between us, in the public eye.

Could I let that happen to the team? One thing that was sure, I felt really insignificant right now. I had some thinking to do. I had to put my team and the woman I loved first, before myself.

Even if it meant ripping my heart out of my own chest and stomping it into the ice.

Chapter Twenty-Five

Andi

THIS MORNING'S MEETING WITH THE TEAM'S manager and the CFO went well. They were both men. Both receptive to my presence here, as far as I could tell.

At any rate, they hadn't been rude or condescending. That was a good sign. They were dedicated to the team, that was what mattered. That would be the glue that held us altogether.

I pushed in earbuds and put on the latest album from Jack Clutterbuck, my favorite pop singer, before opening my email and checking for anything important.

After deleting several requests from Nigerian princes to send me large sums of money, I moved on to actual email. None of which was too urgent. I moved them into folders and sat at my desk, grooving quietly to the music.

A hint of movement in the doorway caught my eye, stopping me mid-groove.

A giant teddy bear appeared, held up by male hands.

A slow smile crept onto my face. I remembered Cam suggesting he win one for me at the pier before we went on the rollercoaster instead. He must have decided I needed one anyway.

I pulled out my earbuds and tossed them onto the desk. Smiling, my heart racing, I rose and stepped towards the teddy bear.

"He's adorable."

"Of course he is." The voice behind the bear made me freeze. A moment later, the plush animal was lowered, revealing a familiar, but not so welcome, face.

"Xander." I should have noticed his sleeves. He wore an expensive suit, not a sweatshirt. I hadn't looked past the large brown teddy. I'd seen what I wanted to see, not what was really there.

Although, I should have anticipated my ex-boyfriend turning up unannounced like this. Just when life was going well, he appeared to remind me of past screw-ups.

"What are you doing here?"

His hair was slightly longer, but his chin was perfectly smooth as always. His eyes, brown with a hint of green, always held a hint of superiority. Like whatever I knew, he knew just that bit more. It was always there, but I hadn't noticed it until now.

"Andi, you look lovely." He placed the teddy on the couch and moved to kiss my cheek before I could step away. "I thought it was time we talked."

I retreated back a couple of feet. "I don't know what we have to talk about."

Now that he wasn't hidden behind a teddy bear, I could see the perfectly tailored navy suit, crisp white shirt and perfectly knotted silk tie. He was a couple of inches shorter than Cam, with a more slender build.

He was undeniably handsome, but to look at him now, I couldn't remember why I was attracted to him.

He gave a short laugh. "Of course we do. I'm sure you've had a lot of time to think during our break."

I frowned at him. "Break? You left. Without saying a single word about it to me. One day you were there and the next you weren't." I gestured from one side of me, to the other. "What was there to think about? You made your feelings abundantly clear."

He stepped towards me. "Evidently, I should have come sooner. Although, I would have thought you'd reach out to me."

"Why would I have done that?" I stood my ground. I wasn't going to let him intimidate me.

"You must have understood why I did it." He seemed genuinely confused.

"Because you didn't want to be with me anymore." I raised my left shoulder and dropped it. "Why else would you leave without a word?"

"I wanted you to realize what we had. What life apart would be like," he said. "Now you've experienced it, it's time to end our break. Before you do something you might regret."

Was that what this was about? He'd seen the photos of me and Cam and came crawling back now he realized someone else wanted me.

"What might I regret?" I said, my tone icy. "Moving on with my life? Discovering that you and I were over a long, long time ago? My only regret was not ending it before you did."

He clicked his tongue. "Don't be ridiculous, Andi. If you need a little more time, I can give you another week or two. But you have to understand that if anyone sees you with someone else again, it will reflect badly on me."

I stared at him. I shouldn't even be slightly surprised that the only thing he gave a shit about was his reputation.

"What Cam and I do is none of your business," I said. "You made that abundantly clear when you packed up and left."

"People are talking, Andi," he said warningly. "People I work with are talking about me behind their hands. They knew we were together and planned to have a life with each other, and now you're off doing fuck knows what with some...hockey player. Do you have any idea how that looks? It's impacting my next promotion. The partners are concerned my girlfriend might cause a scandal."

"Good thing I'm not your girlfriend then," I snapped. "Did you bother to inform them of that? Or did you assure them you'd come here and I'd fall in line? Be the dutiful wife like my mother is? Sit around and knit, and wait for you to come home at the end of a long day so I can place a hot meal in front of you?"

"Why not?" He lifted his rounded chin. "You could work for a while if you want to. I know how much you like being busy. When the babies come—"

I gaped at him. "Xander, there will be no babies. Not between you and me."

Had he lost his ever loving mind? He must have if he thought we had a future together.

"The best thing you ever did was leave. The moment you stepped out the door, you ended it. It hurt for a little while, but I got over it. I realized it was for the best. For me. For you too, I guess. Now you can find someone who fits in with your nineteen fifties housewife ideal. That sure as hell isn't me."

I'd lose my shit in the first day or two.

"It was never meant to be an end, Andi," he insisted. "Like I said, it was a break. I'm not sure what's gotten into you. It must be this place. That hockey player has some kind of influence over you, doesn't he? He has you convinced that the future we planned isn't what you want."

He shook his head slowly. "I know you better than that. *You're* better than that." He closed his eyes for a minute and shook his head, like he was trying to get through to a three-year-old.

"You know people like that don't stick around with one woman for long. The first pretty face that crosses their path and they're off, chasing them like a dog in heat." He opened his eyes. "Don't say you don't know that's true. We both know it is."

From what I'd seen, for some of the players, it was, but not for all of them. Not for Cam. He wasn't out to chase pussy.

I shook my head. "You're wrong. That's just a stereotype. Lots of the guys on the team are happily married with children. Committed. They wouldn't look sideways at another woman."

"They may not, but what about Cameron North?" Xander sneered. "That's his name, isn't it? He seems to keep some dubious company. How many additional endorsements has he received since that incident on the rollercoaster? I'd imagine several, all very lucrative."

My eyes twitched towards my computer. Several of those emails were regarding endorsement deals for Cam. A couple of them were worth millions. A few of those and he could comfortably retire. But he would have gotten those anyway, wouldn't he? Not because of any relationship with me.

"I see I'm right." Xander looked smug. "He's doing nothing but using you, and preying on how vulnerable you are right now. I must take some of the blame for that. I should have come to you before he tried anything with you. But I'm here now and we can deal with him. You can file a sexual harassment lawsuit against him. He'll have to..."

He continued talking, but I barely heard him over the blood that roared through my ears.

Was it possible Cam was using me to benefit his own career? I didn't want to consider it, but those endorsement deals told me I had to. The timing was too convenient.

I thought back to how he found me sitting on the bench by the beach. He'd insisted we go to the pier. What if none of that was spontaneous?

What if he knew where to find me and where to take me so we could be seen together? He could have planted the person that took those photos. Hell, he could have recruited his sister to help him. She could have influenced the camera operator to film me eating that hotdog. To generate more publicity around us.

Would he have deliberately humiliated me like that? He couldn't have known I might choke but he might have invited the scrutiny, and the rumors that surfaced after that.

I sat back on the edge of my desk and rubbed my temples. Too many thoughts were thundering around in my brain. Too many insecurities and questions.

I'd wanted so badly to believe him when he told me he was falling in love with me. Was that another part of the plan? Pretty words to suck me in deeper?

I reminded myself that he didn't fuck me when he could have, but the ugliest of my insecurities suggested that was because he didn't want to. Pretending to care about me was one thing, but subjecting his body to mine was another.

"What was with the bear?" The words popped out before I could even think them.

Xander stopped mid-sentence and looked confused.

I repeated the question and nodded toward the teddy bear that sat on the couch watching us, probably judging me. Why wouldn't he? I was certainly judging myself.

"It was delivered to the reception desk near the front door," Xander finally said. "I said I was coming this way anyway and I'd bring it up for you."

"You didn't buy it for me," I stated.

"Of course not." He looked as though that was the most ridiculous idea he ever heard. "Why would I waste money on something like that?"

"I have no idea," I said. "It didn't seem like something you'd do."

"Of course not," he said again, like I'd just paid him a compliment. "Now—"

"I have to thank you," I interrupted. "The time we had together was…interesting. We had some good times in the early days. But you packing up and leaving was a wake-up call. It was a reminder that I should be out living my best life. That isn't with you. It never was and never will be. I honestly wish you happiness. Whatever that means to you."

"Andi." He put out a hand to me, but must have seen the expression on my face. He realized I was not only serious, but done. Done with him and his judgment. Done with any plans he thought we should have. Done standing here wasting time talking to him.

He lowered his hand. "If you ever change your mind…"

"I won't. But if you need a friend, maybe we can be that some day." Spontaneously, I stepped forward and gave him a quick hug.

Over his shoulder, I saw Cam step into the doorway. He saw me standing with my arms around Xander, and turned and walked away.

Chapter Twenty-Six

Cam

I KNEW WHAT I WANTED TO SAY TO HER. I'D rehearsed the words in my head over and over. I had everything nailed down tighter than a play in the last half of a play-off game. I was going to tell her everything that went through my mind in the last twenty-four hours.

But then, stepping into the doorway and seeing her with him, everything went right out of my head. I felt as though someone slapped the puck so hard it flew past all the seats and smashed through the wall of the arena.

I don't know, maybe it ended up in the ocean, before sinking under the waves. Whatever, it was not in my brain anymore.

The only thing in there now was her and

Xander. Yeah, I'd looked him up after she mentioned him the other day. He was exactly the kind of man a woman like her would go for. The kind she'd be expected to marry and have children with. Solid, reliable, rich. Boring as fuck.

I hurried towards the elevator. I pressed the down button before deciding to take the stairs instead. I didn't want to linger here any longer than necessary.

I'd seen her beautiful blue eyes looking at me over that other guy's shoulder. She might decide to come after me. If she did, I needed to be somewhere else right now.

If I was stuck in an elevator with her, I'd change my mind. I'd never go through with what was now running through my brain. I'd pin her to the elevator wall, slide my hands up her skirt and make her come so hard she forgot her name.

"Cam!" I heard her call out before the door closed behind me.

I wanted to glance back, but I kept trotting down the stairs, barely paying attention to where I was going.

I pushed out at the bottom and headed to the street. I hurried through the crowds and over to the promenade on the opposite side of the road from the arena.

There, I sat down on the sand and waited.

It didn't take her long, and she was puffing lightly, when she sat down beside me.

"It's not what you thought," she said.

"What did I think?" I looked over at her. She was so fucking gorgeous it hurt. Her cheeks were pink and her curls were particularly unruly. She was definitely wrong when she said nothing was cuter than a basket of kittens. She was.

She frowned, confused at the expression on my face. Or maybe I had food on my cheek. No, it was definitely the expression.

"I thought maybe you thought I got back together with him," she said slowly. "But you don't think that, do you?"

"Fuck no," I said. "I know how we feel about each other. I figured you needed some space to make it clear that he's not a part of your life any more."

She let out a soft breath and her eyes shone. "I called your name."

"I figured it would be better to get some air out here," I said. "Firstly, so I didn't punch what's his name for being anywhere near my woman. Secondly, because—" I spread my hands and gestured out at the beach and the people walking and enjoying the late autumn sunshine. "I figured it was past time we were seen in public again. You know, so everyone knows you're my girlfriend."

I leaned over to wipe a tear from her cheek. "Why are you crying?"

"Because Xander tried to convince me you were only with me for the endorsements, but then I realized something. He would have said anything to get under my skin." She sniffed. "And he never would have sent me a teddy bear."

"You got that, hmmm?" I smiled softly. "I still want to win one for you, but I figured in the meantime he'd do. He's kinda cute, don't you think?"

She smiled. "Not as cute as you. But thank you, that was very sweet."

"You're sweet," I told her. "For the record, it never occurred to me that being with you would lead to additional endorsement offers. I don't care about shit like that. All I care about is you."

"I know," she said. "I second-guessed everything for a few moments, then I remembered how you looked at me when you told me you were falling in love with me. Nothing in my life has ever felt so real."

I leaned over and whispered, "I might have lied.

I'm not falling in love with you, Andi Welling. I'm already head over heels in love with you. I think I have been since that first night in Shells, but I was too scared, or too dumb, to figure it out. I think I always knew you weren't a puck bunny."

"I'm more of a puck nerd," she said with a laugh.

I grinned. "Me too. I'll also accept puck geek."

"I love you, puck geek," she said.

I pressed my forehead to hers. "I love you too, puck nerd. You make me feel alive, like no one else ever has. I want you in my life forever. Maybe a bit longer. I mean, I've seen Supernatural. How many times did those guys come back to life?"

She didn't tell me that might not be how it worked, she just kissed me like there was no one in the world but us.

"You make me feel beautiful," she whispered.

"You are beautiful." I slid my tongue across her lower lip. "I want to show you just how much."

"I know you mentioned us being seen out in public," she said slowly.

I chuckled against her mouth. "Some things are better kept behind closed doors."

We barely made it through the door of my apartment before we started to tear off each other's clothes. My hands were under her blouse, pushing it up over her head and letting it float to a puddle on the floor.

I kicked the door shut, pressed her back against it and kissed her, tasting her mouth and tongue.

"I want you so much," I whispered.

"I want you too." She slid her hands up my sweatshirt and over my flat stomach to caress the muscles of my chest.

Holding her in place with one hand, I grabbed the hem of my shirt and pulled it up and off.

She cocked her head at me. "Are you real? You feel real." She poked her finger into my chest.

I grinned. "I'm definitely real." To prove it, I unhooked her bra, freeing her glorious breasts, before I leaned down to draw her nipple between my lips and suck.

She moaned, the sound almost enough to make me come way too soon.

I gripped her ass and carried her into my bedroom. I undid her skirt, and pulled it down her legs, before doing the same to her emerald green panties.

I sat in front of her, admiring her beautiful pussy and dark red curls. "So fucking gorgeous." I lay down between her luscious thighs and tasted her pussy with the tip of my tongue. "Delicious."

"Cam," she whispered. That was all she said in words, after that she spoke in moans, pants and soft sighs, while I slid my fingers into her wet heat and fucked her with my mouth and tongue.

I marveled at the way she writhed and trembled the closer she got. Finally, she shattered on my tongue, calling out my name as her whole body flushed pink. I went on licking her, drawing out her orgasm for as long as I could, before she finally sank back down to the mattress.

"Wow," she whispered. "That was—"

"Just the beginning." I shed my pants and reached over to my dresser to grab a condom.

"Can I put that on?" she asked.

When I handed her the packet, she pushed me onto my back, tore it open with her teeth and rolled the condom down my length. Her hands were gentle, but her eyes were huge. "You're so big," she whispered.

She straddled my thighs and lowered herself down onto me, bit by bit until I was buried all the way inside her.

"Fucking hell, Andi," I said. "You feel like heaven." I locked my eyes on her. "You feel like home."

"You'll make me cry again," she said. She placed her hands on my chest and pushed herself up and down my cock, her beautiful breasts bouncing with each movement.

I'd never seen such an incredible sight in my life. For once, my cock, balls, the back of my brain, and the front were in complete agreement.

And so was my heart. Every part of me loved every part of her.

I gripped her hips and thrust up slowly, wanting to make this first time last. Time stopped and all that was left was our bodies, in perfect unison. Nothing else in the world mattered.

And then she was shattering around me again, and I lost myself inside her, roaring at the bliss that surged through me. The very last of any walls between us were washed away in our mutual pleasure. Gone as we made love to each other. Knowing this was just the first time.

Knowing we'd have forever.

Epilogue 1

Andi

"CAN YOU BELIEVE IT'S BEEN A YEAR?" I squeezed Cam's hand as we made our way through the glittering crowds at the charity gala. It was basically a Who's Who of Lowball Bay. All of the Sea Dragons were here, all dressed in tuxedos. Many with partners, others not. All of the coaches and a lot of the staff were here too.

They were joined by the richest and most influential people in the city. Including Harman Fields, the owner of the Lowball Bay Sea Cucumbers MLB team. I'd worked with him in the past and considered him a friend.

Rafe, who was hovering around near the drink table with Jacoby, was ecstatic. His idea of revenge for drawing on them was season tickets to all the Sea

Dragons home games, for life. Considering what he might have done, I got off lightly.

"It feels like a week," Cam said. "At the same time, it feels like a lifetime. Don't look now, but your mother is coming over here."

I suppressed a groan and forced a smile instead. "Mom." I kissed her cheek and to my surprise, she kissed mine.

"Andrea, you're practically glowing." She leaned back and smiled at us both.

Some things would never change.

I put a finger to my lips. "It's too early to tell everyone yet."

She waved a hand at me. "It'll be time soon enough. As for you," she raised her eyebrows at Cam.

"Yes, Mom?" He'd taken to calling her that teasingly, but she hadn't told him to stop. I think she secretly liked it.

She looked at him down her nose.

He raised his finger in the air. "Right. I knew there was something I'd forgotten."

I frowned at him. "What is it? Did we forget to order enough punch?"

He grinned and sank to one knee as he pulled something out of his pocket.

My lips dropped apart at the sight of a small black box in his hand. "You didn't?"

He shrugged. "I figured I would, after all the hard work you've put into tonight." He took my hand. "In case you hadn't noticed, I'm crazy about you. Since we met, my life has been better. So much more than I ever could have asked for. Some days, I wonder if I deserve you, but I'd like to spend the rest of my life trying to prove that I do. Will you marry me?"

I blinked away a haze of tears and nodded. "Of course I will. I'd like nothing more than to be your wife."

"It's about time," Mom muttered. "I had my doubts about him, but he's changed my mind. Welcome to the family, Cameron."

Her blessing was a start. We'd have to work on the rest of it later.

I let him slip the ring on my finger and pulled him to his feet so I could kiss him. I didn't care who saw. Let everyone watch and know that he was mine.

Now and forever.

Epilogue 2

Andi

I LOOKED UP WHEN A SHADOW STEPPED INTO MY office doorway.

"Dad. This is unexpected."

Quentin waved me down before I stood, and strode over to sit in a chair opposite me.

"Is Mom okay?" Why else would he be here?

"We've been arguing a bit lately," he said softly.

"You're always arguing," I said. "Is that why you gave me the team? So you wouldn't fight over me anymore?"

"It isn't just you we fight over," he said. "We also argue over your sister. And the color your mother wants to paint the bathroom. Sunshine yellow, for the record."

"I can't see my mother in a bathroom painted sunshine yellow," I remarked.

"That's what I keep telling her. I think she wants to do it to spite me. The moment the paint is dry, she'll choose a shade of white. And I'll let her. You know why? Because that's what love is."

"Letting someone make a choice you know they'll hate and then watching them fix it?" I asked.

"In a manner of speaking," he said. "Letting people make their own choices and being there for them if things don't work out. And cheering them on when they do. That was why I gave you the team. I wanted you to make your own choices. Working with me... I was all too aware you weren't able to do that. Everything goes past me."

He was right about that. Nothing went on in Welling without his knowledge and approval.

Quietly, he added, "It was time for you to have somewhere everything goes past *you*."

"I didn't realize you'd had so much faith in me." I was trying not to get choked up with emotion.

This was the first time he gave any indication he truly believed in me and what I could do. Sure, he'd hired me and I'd worked my way up, but he'd never said he was proud of me. Never gave me any kind of special attention or treatment. I hadn't wanted any, but his approval meant everything.

"Andi, you're one of my proudest accomplishments. You and your sister. Welling Developments comes a distant third. Anything either of you do, I have faith that you'll succeed. Because you're as smart and as stubborn as your mother."

"She still thinks I'm a kid," I said ruefully.

"Give her some time," he said. "She's always had difficulty cutting the apron strings when it comes to you girls. Especially you. Pia picked up a pair of scissors and snipped them, but you've always been closer to your mother. Always willing to bend to make amends, even when she's in the wrong."

"I'm a doormat," I concluded.

He chuckled and patted my knee. "Definitely not a doormat. More like a peacemaker. Exactly what a good CEO needs to be. You listen to every side and understand it before looking for a compromise everyone can live with. I don't know too many people who can do that. Much less do it well. When the time comes, you'll take Welling to places I couldn't dream of. Now, I better get back to the office before they decide it's time to hand the company to you." He leaned over and kissed my cheek before stepping out the door.

Thank you so much for reading! If you loved Cam and Andy's story, please leave a review.

What's next for the Sea Dragons? It's time for Nate and Oaklyn's story in Personal as Puck.

Click here for a bonus scene of Cam trying to win that teddy for his woman.

About the Author

Freya M. Love writes steamy romantic comedies with guys we like to swoon over and women we can relate to. All wrapped up with a snort-worthy bow that comes with no guarantee you won't spit out your drink.

Join the fun of Freya's Lovlies on Facebook! Join!
Subscribe to my Newsletter.
Follow me on Pinterest.
Follow me on TikTok.
Follow me on Amazon.
Follow me on Bookbub.

Also by Freya M. Love

Lowball Bay Sea Dragons

Not the Puck Bunny

Personal as Puck

Influential as Puck

For the Love of Puck

Lowball Bay Humpbacks

Game Plan

Playing Field

Offside

Goal Line